COSCOM ENTERTAINMENT

OTHER FICTION

A STRANGER DEAD
A RED DARK NIGHT
APRIL (WRITING AS PETER FOX)
MAGIC MAN (DELUXE CHAPBOOK)
THE WAY OF THE FOG (THE ARK OF LIGHT VOL. 1)
DEVIL'S PLAYGROUND (WITH KEITH GOUVEIA)
ON HELL'S WINGS (WITH KEITH GOUVEIA)
ZOMBIE FIGHT NIGHT: BATTLES OF THE DEAD
MAGIC MAN PLUS 15 TALES OF TERROR
UNDENIABLE
THE DANCE OF MERVO AND FATHER CLOWN
FLASH ATTACK: THRILLING STORIES OF TERROR, ADVENTURE, AND
INTRIGUE
GIGANTI-GATOR DEATH MACHINE: TRIPLE FEATURE
ZOMTROPOLIS: A RECORD OF LIFE IN A DEAD CITY

ANTHOLOGIES (AS EDITOR)

DEAD SCIENCE
ELEMENTS OF THE FANTASTIC
VICIOUS VERSES AND REANIMATED RHYMES: ZANY ZOMBIE
POETRY FOR THE UNDEAD HEAD
METAHUMANS VS THE UNDEAD
BIGFOOT TERROR TALES VOL. 1 (WITH ERIC S. BROWN)
BIGFOOT TERROR TALES VOL. 2 (WITH ERIC S. BROWN)
METAHUMANS VS WEREWOLVES

NON-FICTION

BOOK MARKETING FOR THE
FINANCIALLY-CHALLENGED AUTHOR
CANADIAN SCRIBBLER: COLLECTED LETTERS OF AN
UNDERGROUND WRITER
LOOK, UP ON THE SCREEN! THE BIG BOOK OF
SUPERHERO MOVIE REVIEWS
GETTING DOWN AND DIGITAL:
HOW TO SELF-PUBLISH YOUR BOOK
THE CANISTER X TRANSMISSION: YEAR ONE

The Canister X Transmission: Year Two
The Canister X Transmission: Year Three
The Canister X Transmission: Year Four
The Canister X Transmission: The Long Year Five
The Canister X Transmission: The Very Long Year Six
The Canister X Transmission: Year Seven

POETRY

The Hand I've Been Dealt
Haunted Melodies and Other Dark Poems
Still About A Girl
Caught in Black Headlights

WWW.CANISTERX.COM

by

A.P. FUCHS

COSCOM ENTERAINMENT

WINNIPEG

ISBN 978-1-83436-008-9

Published by Coscom Entertainment

Text set in Garamond
Printed and bound in the USA

Cover art by Kevin Phillips
Cover design by A.P. Fuchs

For those who have a vision. For those who see it
through no matter what it takes.

To those who become that which they are meant to be.

BATTLE OF POWER TRILOGY BOOK THREE

AXIOM-MAN™

NEW DAWN

Prologue

The void.

It was endless. Every direction Redsaw looked was a mosaic of red and black clouds that went on for an eternity. As much as he couldn't see an end to it, there was this sense it carried a depth—a physical one—that, should he decide to explore, would swallow him whole and he'd never find his way out.

None of that mattered anyway. What he wanted had been right in front of him: Axiom-man, robbed of power.

Before flying here into the Doorway of Darkness, Redsaw had wanted to snatch Axiom-man's power, somehow absorb it. But something wasn't right. There had been . . . two of him. For less than a microsecond, the shape of a man flashed as quickly as a lightbulb sparking out. But Redsaw saw him. Was it Axiom-man's soul leaving his body and because of his power, for a brief moment, it manifested itself in humanoid form before vanishing into the afterlife? Would Axiom-man's power naturally drift back to where it came from, never to be obtained, or was it, for a split second, something that could have been grabbed?

Or, maybe, the power shift occurred within a blink and now, here, in the Doorway of Darkness, Redsaw had Axiom-man's power within him. All he needed to do was access it.

Redsaw hovered there in the void and tried to summon energy into his eyes the same way he gathered it into his hands before release. Yet no matter how hard he focused, he could not create the same sensation, the same *knowing*, a power release was about to occur.

"It has ended," came a voice from all directions. The master.

Redsaw knew he had to be respectful when he spoke lest he be set in his place. But that was only for now. As long as his master couldn't read his mind, he could control the situation and do and say what he had to before somehow syphoning his master's power for himself. "My lord, are you certain?" He thought back to the bright flash of a man before flying into the Doorway.

"I am not to be questioned. Your adversary is no more. When this realm was revealed unto him again, it was ensured he would know it. Your mind is so limited. You think here is the end. You think this place is just that: this place. No. It is that and more. It reaches, it searches, it moves. This realm had access to your plane in space-time and reached your adversary, taking what is rightfully mine."

Rightfully? Redsaw thought.

"He was vanquished," his master said.

That man. Redsaw still didn't know what he saw, and he was also unsure if what his master said was true. What if it had indeed been Axiom-man's soul leaving his body? Worse, his power? "Do you have them? His powers?"

"I have what I need, and you did what you were required to do. What is it you want?"

Though still floating, Redsaw folded into a kneeling position and bowed his head. "I don't want him to be a threat ever again. If his abilities died with him, so be it, but if they have lingered, I want them."

"And what will you do with them?"

Redsaw raised his head. "Turn the world to you."

CHAPTER ONE

Two years later.

Owen Tower stood over what was left of Winnipeg, the Doorway of Darkness open wide above it.

Redsaw seldom left the roof and the throne of silver he constructed for himself. From here, his seat of power, elevated on a silver platform with over thirty steps leading up to it, the city could be viewed in full in all directions.

Above, the sky was a swirling mix of black and red clouds that continuously poured upward from the Doorway of Darkness as a never-ending beacon of authority over the city. Charges of powerful red energy spewed from all corners of the Doorway, periodically zapping Redsaw's throne. Each time they struck, a surge of power went through him. He tested it before and each zap gave him a temporary surge of power.

The sound of a low, angry bell rang across the roof. Redsaw looked toward the rooftop entrance that led down into the rest of the building. This bell was for one thing and one thing only. The door was purposefully unlocked because it was widely known throughout the city that to even attempt contact with Redsaw without permission would cost you your head.

The door swung open and three men filed onto the roof. First was a tall, thick man in red and black leather followed by a man wearing a tailored white suit with black shirt, white tie, and white fedora, all beneath an open white overcoat, then in leather behind him another stocky but powerful man taking up the rear.

The two men in leather guided the man in the white suit to the bottom of the steps leading up to Redsaw's throne. Redsaw eyed the man in the fedora. One of the men in leather gave the man in white a nudge.

"Hail Redsaw king," the man in white said.

"Have you come to offer tribute?" Redsaw asked.

"I have, my lord." The man in white clearly looked uncomfortable and the expression on his face, even from thirty steps away, was evident: He did not like this.

But Redsaw did. The humiliation, the lording of authority, the clear message the mob had lost its hold on the city and all gangs now answered to him. "Leave it."

"Yes sir," the man said.

The man in leather gave him another nudge.

"Yeah, yeah, get off me," the man in white said. He produced a large black velvet bag from inside his coat. It was about the size of shoebox and the man in white almost seemed relieved to unburden it despite what it represented. He laid the bag down at the foot of the steps.

"Thank you for your loyalty," Redsaw said.

The man straightened good and tall then bowed before him. This was the best part, the submission. Just as soon as the gesture was made, the two men in leather each took hold of the man's shoulders and showed him the way off the roof and back to the door. It was only when the three men were gone did Redsaw descend the steps, each footfall done with deliberate care. When he reached the bottom, he scooped up the bag and moved back to his seat of power.

He pulled on the drawstring that kept the velvet bag shut and opened it. Inside, the bag was filled with small silver bars, each about two inches by four and about an inch thick. While demanding gold was not outside his authority, silver was the metal of choice thanks to its conductive power and its ability to adapt to the energy Redsaw produced.

It was a requirement each bag contain an even number of bars for simple division by two. Half was reserved for construction. The other half was designated for resources. While the original construction of the Doorway on this roof bankrupted Redsaw, his losses were quickly recovered within a few months of his reign. Everything since then was used for reserve and to farm out various errands, some deadly. A bar of silver went a long way with a small-time crook. Even a middle-of-the-road career class criminal. Working for a single bar or possibly two, instantly made those hired obedient to him and his wants. He learned a long time ago as Oscar Owen money made the world go around and the more of it you had, the faster you could make it spin, and the faster you made it spin, eventually, placed you in a position where you were the only one who could slow the momentum thus gaining leverage above others.

As for men like the man in the white fedora, Redsaw was generous. He knew the mob needed to remain well-funded, so there was no sense in demanding every dime they took in. Twenty-percent tribute was all that was required. They could run off the rest.

Twenty percent. Double the standard tithe from religious folks.

After all, he was a god.

———

Jack Gunn had had multiple opportunities to leave the city over the past couple of years. There was a mass exodus of panic when the Doorway first opened. It didn't last long. Citywide, the effects of the Doorway's open presence led to slow deterioration of Winnipeg's physical infrastructure. It was as if concrete and steel girders weren't built to withstand the constant presence of such a powerful force that emanated its strength like a thick blanket over every street. Building exteriors were cracked from the open Doorway. One building crumbled to the ground when its interior beams and supports weakened simply by being in close proximity to the Doorway.

This was no longer Winnipeg. No longer the city Gunn had sworn to protect, and his ally in blue, the only man who may have known how to stop this, was gone.

Gunn ground his teeth and furrowed his brow. "Thanks a lot, blue boy. You were supposed to fix this. Get the guy out. Instead, you went off and died on everybody." His facial muscles relaxed and a tear pricked the corner of his eye, but not for Axiom-man.

For the city.

There was no hope here. When Redsaw set up his kingdom, it was quickly made clear to the outside world the city was his and outside interference would not be tolerated. Gunn still remembered that day. Probably so did a lot of other folks who didn't make it out.

The jets, the helicopters, the marching of troops toward the city, men in full military garb coming in proud to exterminate the threat. Instead, a wild red streak flew out from between the buildings and immediately solid beams of red power struck down the planes, first one by slicing off its wing, another by a direct blast to the engine, another to a set of helicopter blades that melted and drooped and took the whole chopper down.

Those on the ground moved as fast as they could both on foot and in vehicles. A barrage of red fire rained from the heavens and blasted gaps into the organized invasion, removing men in explosions of blood and body parts. Tanks and jeeps detonated with direct blasts to their gas tanks. The supply wagons loaded with weapons were left alone for raiding later.

Gunn recalled a season where every man and woman on the street had a firearm, both for protection and to get what they wanted. He even saw a few kids running around with pistols and watched in horror as a young girl playfully pointed a gun at a panicked man and pulled the trigger. When he dropped dead, the shrill of her scream embedded itself into Gunn's memory like a nail driven deep into a block of wood.

There was no place for cops. Those remaining, who were in uniform, were quickly killed as the mobs and gangs took anything and everything they wanted, whoever was in their way be damned. Of those who worked undercover, a large majority were found out and executed one by one at Redsaw's feet. There were still a few good men and women officers peppered throughout the city, but no one spoke to each other nor gave way to giving up their occupation. As much as Gunn wanted his hands on things to bring things back into order, he knew he couldn't. So those of the law remained unknown, and he had to trust they would assist when and where needed because right now the city needed its heroes and those few men and women were it.

That night two years ago at the foot of Owen Tower changed everything. Though Gunn couldn't see the full picture from ground level nor was he able to ascend to its top after the fact, he realized Oscar Owen and Redsaw worked together. There was no other explanation for Redsaw to have chosen Owen Tower other than to perhaps humiliate Oscar, even kill him, before taking over. But it made sense now.

"And you're an idiot for not figuring it out sooner," Gunn said. Even now, here, the guilt and regret of being so fixated on Axiom-man's activities instead of on Redsaw's ate away at him. It was so obvious and the guy slipped right past him. It was a single item of deductive reasoning and he completely overlooked it. One thing: Redsaw had to get his resources from somewhere and while everything could easily have been stolen, there was the issue of storage. Bags of cash could only pile up so high, and Redsaw didn't seem the type to disperse his resources across multiple locations. Granted, he probably could have hired out the guarding of his supply and would gain obedience lest there be deadly consequences, but it didn't fit the profile of a megalomaniac. It would also explain the rapid rate at which Oscar Owen gained his wealth. The man was a nobody until several years back. Gunn had looked into his file, the little they knew about him anyway. Born poor, raised poor, worked a low-paying job until lucking out and getting some cash from some side endeavors. While this by itself raised no alarm, the bell sounded when more and more endeavors were pursued more quickly than your average businessman. And with how quickly Owen Tower was built, it had been done in half the time a normal building would take.

All these pieces. All these clues. All these things that slipped right under Jack's nose because he was too concerned about another man in a cape that was actually on his side.

Winnipeg's fall was his fault, too.

There was only one question: What was next?

CHAPTER TWO

THE FOX AND Hounds Tavern had been a wonderful pub some years back. Rustic interior, a wooden bar, wooden tables and chairs, simple carpeting, plenty of beer on tap, and the constant music of rock and roll on the airwaves. It was one of those places that was *human*, a place to go when things were either looking up or looking down. A place where you could be yourself without judgment and just enjoy a pint while you process your day.

Now, there was no sign hanging outside the door. The windows were boarded up with particle board, the beer no longer flowed, and half the furnishings were overturned. No electricity or running water.

Three candles lit the room, each placed equidistant from each other along the long, oak table. A set of three occupied wooden chairs were on each side of the table along with a chair at the head and foot.

The men gathered around. Here, in this abandoned place, they were safe from anyone looking for them or just anyone looking to cause trouble. The meetings never took place in the same place twice to avoid tracking, but tonight, there was business to discuss.

The man in the white fedora and white suit sat at the head slowly sipping a small glass of moonshine and smoking a cigar. The others at the table were not dressed nearly as elegantly, but some still had on suits while others were in scruffy street clothes that appeared to have not seen the wash in months. But tonight wasn't about appearances.

All present at the table looked to the man in the fedora. The rule was you didn't speak until after he did.

The man took a long drag off his cigar, blew out some of the smoke in a smooth, thick stream then formed a few smoke rings at the end, little halos to demonstrate not all was lost.

His name was Charlie. No one knew his last name and he liked it fine that way. And it was Charlie. Not Charles or Chuck. Charlie. Anything else was an insult. However, he did let Charlie Brown slide now and then out of amusement and the association was actually an assist in making him appear slightly weak when that was far from the truth. Good ol' Charlie Brown presented a persona not nearly as deadly as simply Charlie.

Charlie took a small sip of moonshine, let it slide slowly along his tongue and down his throat. As his lungs warmed, he set the cigar down on the side of the ashtray then turned to the men.

Never known for introductions or opening with a general outline or plan, Charlie cut right to it: "We are incurring additional costs in our operation. *My* operation . . . as well as yours. It is most . . . unfortunate . . . that we have to interact. Foes now friends. Enemies now pals. No, that is not true. No one here is a friend to the other." The men glanced around the table at each other, each face stoic with a hint of anger. "But we are here. Again. Once more having to hide lest these talks be discovered. Bottom line, gentlemen, our options for producing silver are running thin thus our . . . converters . . . are increasing their fee. All that cash you have, you might as well burn a portion of it and consider it a loss. All we had to do was maintain control and each one of you . . . including myself, sadly admitted . . . lost it. A couple years ago this city was a playground and each of us gained more than we had before things began to burn. Before that clown in red and black decided to run the show." He slammed his fist on the table. All glasses no matter how full rattled from the vibration. "It has to stop."

Black Jimmy slowly raised a hand. Charlie hated it when Jimmy had something to say. "Black Jimmy" was just a moniker. Charlie didn't know his real name nor did he care, but he did care that here he was a Caucasian male in a white suit talking to a black man who decided to put "black" in front of his name as if to emphasize his heritage. While there was nothing wrong with that, the racial undertone also surfaced and Charlie was never sure if Black Jimmy had the name in place so if the racial card was played, he'd have a good excuse to blow someone's head off. But Charlie did admire the manipulation. It was both subtle and overt and certainly worked at forcing someone to choose their words carefully.

Charlie nodded in Jimmy's direction.

"All of us here have had talks. Nothing in depth but enough to agree with your point, but 'it has to stop' is more of a notion than a statement. Statements are firm, concrete, and have something behind it . . . like a plan. Notions do not. At best, they're ideas."

"Are you really going to be a dictionary tonight?"

"You know I love my words. But the real question on everyone's minds," he glanced around the table, "is are you making a statement or just venting a feeling?"

Charlie picked up his cigar then pointed it at Jimmy as if his cigar was a gun. "Not impressed."

"You have yet to give an answer."

He had Charlie there. You could always count on Jimmy to turn the conversation back on you; yet another reason why Charlie hated talking to him.

"We are stuck," Charlie said, tone flat.

"So you don't have a plan."

"No," Charlie said, "but I do have information."

"On Redsaw or more jibber jabber about what's going down on the streets? If the latter, we already have that information."

Charlie went to take a sip of moonshine then retracted his hand. He needed to think clearly for this one. "Your problem, Jimmy, is you cause problems. And you're also short-sighted."

Jimmy grimaced. If this was any other time in the past, a gun would have been pulled out.

"But don't fret because your problems are our solutions," Charlie said.

Jimmy furrowed his brow, obviously not sure where this was going.

Charlie glanced around the table. Each person had a quizzical look on their face. Charlie continued. "Are you all that stupid?"

Two men slid their chairs back and stood as if to assert Charlie should be careful about the next words out of his mouth.

With a wave of his hand, Charlie said, "Sit down, gentlemen. You know you're wasting your time and everyone here is under an alliance until further notice."

"Notice from you?" one of the men said.

"Yes."

The men glared at him but Charlie knew they'd hold their peace. Right now, an alliance was all they had, and no one was going to jeopardize that because it was their only hope to getting back to the way things were.

The men slowly sat down. One put his elbow on the table and leaned his head on his hand as if it suddenly grew too heavy for his neck to hold it up on its own.

"So my 'problems' are your solution? Explain that," Jimmy said.

"What is a problem?" Charlie said. "It's the outcome of a series of events. In other words, it's the solution to an equation. It's an unfavorable solution but a solution nonetheless. So let's backwards engineer and discover where along the equation things became more difficult with our converters."

"I hate semantics," Jimmy said.

"Says the man who takes everything literally."

Jimmy closed his mouth, took a deep breath through his nose and exhaled through the same. "Turning cash and jewels into silver has removed certain . . . abilities . . . because of lack of resources. Our converters know this."

"This is the problem when there is a monopoly on services," Charlie said. "But I do know every man here no longer wishes to pay tribute to our 'king.'"

"So an all-out assault?" It was Vince. Short, Italian, and had no trouble gutting someone if he didn't like even so much as their hairstyle.

"Don't be foolish. What firepower could you possibly have that would ensure his demise?"

Silence at the table.

"Exactly," Charlie said. "We need to look at our problem and work backwards. Somewhere there was a misstep by all of us."

"Hey, I ain't takin' no blame for any of this," Vince said, hands up as if letting go of control. "You're the guy who came along and said that guy in the mask wanted a piece of everything we do and wanted it in silver. Silver bars, to be exact." Vince looked at his hands and then spoke as if talking to his fingers. "Why the guy doesn't do it himself, I don't know. Maybe he doesn't know how or maybe he's too lazy or maybe . . . ."

"He's asserting himself as ruler," Charlie said. "If you can bend the muscle in this town, you can bend or break anything else."

"So the solution?" Jimmy said.

"Is the problem," Charlie said. "We need to talk, all voices heard. We will be civilized with every man allowed to speak. No words will be judged even if the idea is ridiculous. Let's put everything we know in front of us. Our unfavorable equation will surely be in the mix and, from there, we will rewrite the numbers, so to speak, to get an outcome that gets us out from under his thumb."

"Yeah, so you're gonna outthink the guy?" Vince said. "Unless you're a genius, every effort to take him down has failed. Failed real bad. You think you can do better? Even that guy in blue, what's his name, who was probably anyone's best chance at defeating the guy lost. Word for the past couple of years is . . . yeah, that Axiom-man guy . . . was killed in an attempt to take on Redsaw." He ran a hand over his face as if to wipe off the stress. "What a stupid world where people are coming up with fancy codenames. We're not five years old. Sheesh."

"True, Axiom-man failed," Charlie said, "but he was one man. We are many because you all represent a fleet of soldiers."

"Soldiers?" It was the Shark. Won poker every time and the boys at the table stopped playing with him a long time ago because too much was lost. "You can have an army and you still won't stop him. He's fought against any interference from outside authority to infiltrate the city and get him out of the picture. And he's won, guys. Every time. What can we possibly bring to him that would guarantee his end. Heck, you can't even get near him without going up against other freaks with stupid names."

"Calm down," Charlie said. "As mentioned, we need to backwards engineer our position and see where we can adjust course. If we get that right, then the real solution to our issue will present itself. So," he placed his elbow on the table, hands folded under his chin, "let's do some math."

Chapter Three

THE WORLD WAS a big place. Winnipeg was a mere pinprick compared to the globe yet here Redsaw controlled over eight hundred thousand people. Another pinprick compared to the world's population, but stepping back, that *was* a lot of people if you lined them up in a row.

Redsaw sat on his silver throne, gazing up at the Doorway.

This won't last forever, he thought. *Someone, somewhere out there, is thinking about this place. Men and women in think tanks trying to figure out how to put an end to what I've created.* He sighed. Despite his success as Oscar Owen and despite eliminating Axiom-man—even despite having complete control over this city—he was smart enough to know that he wasn't smart enough to know every single angle or approach to anticipating any counter effort. He had the world at bay for the time being, but he had to ensure it'd be kept at bay permanently. The question was how?

He needed an army and not just a local one. The men who held the city in a vice worked for him, and they, more or less, had control over the people. Even a mere stroll down the sidewalk was now viewed as running a gauntlet because your odds of getting mugged were a good eight times out of ten. Most people stayed indoors for this reason. Even local companies made accommodation for folks to work from home for safety and even that work was sporadic. It was more something to do than financial progress. Redsaw insisted through brief contacts with the press that life went on as normal, the only difference of him being at the helm. The control over the local economy, sadly, wasn't as easy as he thought. Too many variables and too many people that to try and line everything up and keep it that way was a fulltime job on its own, a job he didn't have time for and a job he couldn't easily assign.

Everyone was a suspect.

Everyone had the potential to turn on him.

Everyone was still clinging to hope.

Some, even, were still clinging to Axiom-man despite him being gone for the past two years.

There had to be a way to expand Redsaw's control over the city to the entire country, and once over the country, then the continent, and once over the continent, over the world.

But he was one man and despite his power, it wasn't enough to hold it all together. Even if he spent time inside the Doorway of Darkness and even if his master empowered him, he was still only one man versus over eight billion people, many of whom had military resources.

For a brief time when his rule began, there were rumors the entire city would be reduced to nuclear to a wasteland. Then those who thought of that came to their senses and realized slaughtering eight hundred thousand people to get just one man was too extreme.

Him and the world's governments were at a standstill.

But not if he had an army.

Battle Bruiser walked onto the roof. Blood dotted his face from what appeared to be a violent clash. "I ran the checks. All are loyal."

"Are you sure?" Redsaw asked.

He wiped the droplets of blood from his face, smearing them. "I made sure."

"I need you to do something for me."

"Whatever you ask."

"Recruitment."

Battle Bruiser removed his hat, ran his hand through his hair, then put it back on. "All are loyal."

"No, you simpleton. We need . . . everybody."

"Everybody-everybody or just somebodys?"

"Everybody." Redsaw stood from his throne and descended the stairs. "I want them all."

"I'm sorry, boss, but I don't follow. Who's everybody, er, everybody?"

Redsaw shot him a glare. "You know, you're great for muscle but lack in the one strength that counts."

Bruiser checked his biceps then let his arms fall to his sides. "Um . . ."

"Let me tell you in child's terms: I want every citizen of the city to be ready to fight."

"Boss, I don't understand. You run this whole place."

"But glory doesn't last forever."

"I thought you were immortal?"

"How long must I put up with you?" Redsaw muttered. Battle Bruiser wasn't an idiot despite his strength being in his brawn, but his thinking was limited to the streets. Redsaw didn't blame him. You know what you know and that's all you know. "We need to start a war."

"A war? Like, a for-real war?"

"Yes. Not now. Not yet. But I just came up with a plan."

"I'm all ears."

———

Jack Gunn had been over the evidence a thousand times. The problem was, the data he had was incomplete.

He hadn't been on that rooftop that night nor had there been a way to investigate it since Redsaw or one of his meta-powered cronies was always present. All Gunn had was what went down on street level. Pieces of debris, parts of vehicles, weapons—anything he could get his hands on was all reviewed for clues. Fingerprints, which only turned out to be from his own men, leads, giveaways . . . just something to get a start on or get a clue as to Redsaw's full agenda.

Jack had been around criminals long enough in his career to know the smart ones always had a contingency plan or a plan that would further their main plan. With Redsaw, outside of complete domination, there was no plan. At least, nothing Jack could find.

He gazed out the window. Redsaw had this city locked up good and tight. For now, the outside world was kept at bay.

"Yeah, but how long can ya keep it up?" Gunn said and swiped a hand across the papers on the table, sending them to the floor. He stood in the dark in silence and, for a moment, wished a certain blue-caped individual would come in through his window. "But you're gone too and I ain't no spring chicken. I doubt my right hook would stand a chance against that red-and-black costumed freak."

When he signed on to the force decades back, Gunn was all bright-eyed and bushy-tailed, ready to help people and stop some bad guys. Basic training showed him it wasn't as black and white as he'd thought. Years on the job showed him that even when laws were spelled out clear as crystal, even then things could be subject to debate depending on what entered the courtroom. This whole thing was big mess of gray mud. How many people walked free despite evidence to the contrary because of some legal loophole? How many people came through for processing only to be let off in the end or make bail and eventually get absolved of the crime? How many had he locked up over the years and were now out and back to their old ways?

Gunn thought back to Axiom-man. "I should have been more honest with that idiot. Shoulda let him in more. Maybe if I had . . . well, maybe none of this woulda happened." He took a swig of the whiskey from his coffee mug. "Or maybe this was all inevitable and it was only a matter of time before those who could do things I can't would come in and run the show. Survival of the fittest and all that." He took another swig, this one finishing the cup with not nearly enough of a mouthful to be satisfying.

He looked at his badge laying on the coffee table some ten feet away. It was face down on purpose. He had quit the whole thing the second officers got too compliant with their new overlord. Gunn threw his mug at the badge. The mug shattered on impact and Gunn still wished he had thrown it harder.

He went to the window. Though the city was on the prairies, it might as well have been an island.

Gunn wanted help. *Needed* help.

But there was no one to turn to.

Redsaw stood over the dense metal tub filled with silver bars. Each bar was a piece of power but not monetarily. These pieces were for construction, gathered on his master's orders. He just hadn't yet been given the go-ahead to use them nor told in what way.

Silver. The color of coins. The color of money. The color of what got him some earthly power to begin with, never mind the meta power they represented.

He glanced up at the Doorway. Sparks of red energy shot forth in random directions, its edges crackling with the mighty bursts and glows of red lightning.

He had an appointment.

Redsaw glanced at the tub of bars then flew up toward the Doorway. He hovered before it but did not enter. Not yet. Beyond the crackling border was an abyss of red and black clouds, endless and eternal. Once inside, the Doorway was but a mere tiny hole in the grandeur of the other realm.

"Come," his master said.

Redsaw bowed and then floated in. He made sure not to enter too far lest he lose sight of the Doorway so flew in around fifty feet and hovered in the clouds. He glanced around. All over, here, in this endless universe of red and black, was his master. He didn't know if the master was omnipresent or just well-hidden with a voice that echoed across this space. He had never seen him, not since this all began and he wasn't certain if he would ever see him. One day, he hoped, he would, on the day of confrontation. The day he would take his master's mantle and make it his own. But that wouldn't be today.

"You have been assigned this city," his master said. "You have proven yourself worthy for more."

Redsaw tried not to grin so kept his satisfaction to himself. Humility in front of his master was what was expected, so for now, he'd play along. "Thank you, Master." He wanted to ask what other dominion might be his but knew it best to wait for his master to be the one to speak.

"Your territory will extend in full to what these people call a province. You are in a pivotal location, right in the middle of the entire continent. It is here we will form our nucleus and then, from there, expand in a wave to cover to it all."

"My lord, thank you for this privilege. May I ask when this will take effect?"

"Immediately." There was a pause. "You must create a second Doorway."

Redsaw's heart went momentarily hollow then the pang of surprise hit his chest. A *second* Doorway. He didn't know such a thing was possible. Did that mean there was an entrance *and* an exit or did each Doorway serve as both like the one he had now? "Where shall I go to accomplish this?"

"North."

"And what of this portal that sits unguarded?"

"Fool."

Redsaw winced.

"Do you think that I, the occupier of this place, cannot defend that which is mine?"

"No, my lord. Please accept my apologies."

"The Doorway is its own protection for only those tied to the Cosmic can enter. Any born of flesh and blood will perish upon entry because their mortal forms cannot withstand the power of this place."

A swell of pride rose in Redsaw's heart. His powers, his ties to the master, allowed him here unharmed. Though he had been here before, it had only been himself and Axiom-man. And that . . . other being he caught a flash of. He still didn't know who that was but did know his master was very displeased when that figure appeared. Still, the Doorway being its own guard lifted a certain weight inside and excited the challenge of a second Doorway.

Mind racing ahead, wondering if this second Doorway would be the first of many additional Doorways, he couldn't help but say, "We will open all over?"

There was silence. Then, "We will open one." The words were firm.

Okay, don't question. Step by step. You have time. "Yes, Master. Just tell me where to begin."

Charlie removed his white fedora and hung it on the coat rack near the hotel restaurant's door along with his white overcoat. A few feet away, the hostess—a petite brunette dressed in a form-fitting black dress—waited at her greeting station. She glanced at Charlie but didn't say anything as he walked past. He knew she knew he didn't need to be seated. Around the corner was the rest of the gang, all dressed in black suits, black shirts, black ties, hair combed, faces groomed—a display of elegance.

They all stood from their seats while Charlie found his. When he sat down, they sat down.

The waitress came up to him. She did not ask if she could get him anything. It was common knowledge that if Charlie wanted something, he would be the one to ask, not anyone else. "Whiskey. Neat. Quarter glass."

"Yes, sir," she said softly then went off to fetch it.

"We are here, gentlemen, to discuss—"

In a blast of concrete and wooden splinters, the entire side of the room blew open. Charlie and his men dove to the opposite side of the table and hid under it as best they could to avoid the falling debris and get out of some of the dust that floated through the place in a chalky cloud. Every man had his firearm drawn. Charlie had drawn two.

Safeties off, a finger on each trigger, Charlie tried to peek through the murk of dust to see who was—A violent bang rang above his head and the table was launched off all his men as if someone had kicked or hit it into the air. The table flew to the other end of the room and crashed.

Charlie and his men looked up to a moustached man in a domino mask who was built like a tank.

Battle Bruiser.

Charlie knew who he was.

"All right, you louses, listen up. Redsaw wants you to retrieve anyone under your purview and assemble them together under one roof. You want power? This is your chance."

Charlie liked the sound of that but wasn't sure what Bruiser meant. Slowly, he got off the floor and holstered his weapons. His men raised their guns. Charlie put out a hand, gesturing for them to lower them. "Where? Why?"

"I do what I'm told." He reached into his inside jacket pocket and pulled out a folded piece of paper. He opened the page and read: "Gentlemen, for the past two years you have been given free reign over this city to obtain what you want with only a small percentage coming to me. I hope you would agree I have been more than fair. You should also note I have left your operations to your own devices, but if you wish to expand your operations, my devices need to come into play. Your first assignment is a simple one. My associate here" —Bruiser looked up from the page— "that's me. Hehe." He cleared his throat. "My associate here has already informed you what that is. Gather your people. All your people. If there's cost, pay it. It will be worth it in the end. I will be in touch." Battle Bruiser crumpled up the piece of paper and tossed it over his shoulder. "You got yer orders, ya suits. Go and do it. Like the man said, he'll be in touch. I have other stops to make." Bruiser spat on the ground then turned on his heels to exit through the giant hole in the wall. He punched a protruding shard of concrete off one of the walls as he exited.

Charlie took a moment and watched until the man was out of sight.

"So, boss? What say you?"

Charlie reviewed the destruction of the wall. "You heard him. Gather everybody."

CHAPTER FOUR

FOUR SUSPECTS ON foot heading down McDermott, all male and masked, came the voice over the squawk box. Gunn may have been no longer part of the force, but he still kept some toys. The radio was old. All the squad cars had gotten upgrades prior to all this mess so he took it upon himself to snag one for his own use before the others were tossed.

Please send nearest unit. Suspects considered armed and dangerous.

"Don't waste your breath," Gunn said, cigar dangling from his lips. "No one's coming." He took a swig of whiskey from a fresh mug. "Because everyone is afraid!" He hurled the coffee mug of booze across the room. It hit the wall and shattered into a mess of shards and alcohol. "No one in or out. No coming or going." For a brief time, Jack had held out hope that if ground level was under surveillance, there might be the possibility of an assist coming in by air. Plenty of space vertically, was his reasoning. Lots of area to cover. But Redsaw took down any plane entering the airspace over the city. Every. Single. One.

They stopped trying and had given way to the madman.

"Gotta stop obsessing," he told himself. "All angles have been covered. You went deep. You dug through case files looking for tricks and angles and things you didn't think of. No nudges or prompts for new ideas. A basic problem at its core but with a complicated solution." He regretted throwing the whiskey. Now he'd have to haul his keester off the chair, grab yet another new mug from the cupboard, and find wherever he put down the bottle for a refill.

He stood but didn't move. Head bowed, arms loose at his sides, he considered maybe it was time to give up? It was one thing to fight until the death and another to know when to draw the line. He was never good at heavy discernment. Cop stuff? Yeah, he was pretty wise to that and had a reputation for making the right call when everyone else disagreed. It was one of the reasons he was set in charge of the Meta Taskforce. But he was also known for his temper, defiance of authority, and rough-handling of anyone who broke the law.

Gunn was a cop. Justice was the aim. He just wished his former colleagues had the same ideals. Instead, many were bought and paid for to look away while others looked away out of fear. Very few kept going and most of them lost their lives in the pursuit of righting a wrong.

"We're not outmanned," he said quietly. "We're just terribly outgunned."

He'd thought of it all, everything from direct confrontation with Redsaw down to setting a bomb at the base of Owen Tower to level the building. But the place was a fortress, monitored and set on high alert. Once that weird portal opened above the city, after that night of the explosion, many tried to get into the building, to get to the roof only to be met with a barrage of red lightning strikes from above. Bodies dropped with burning holes ripped right through them. Heads were removed and limbs blasted asunder.

There was no getting close enough to Redsaw's fortress. And even if it was somehow possible, what then? Go inside and take the elevator to the roof then have a fist fight? Gunn could only imagine the moment, him stepping out onto the roof, spewing some hate Redsaw's way only to be vaporized in the end.

This was a long game situation, the worst kind to be in. Gunn tracked back in his mind to 1939, the last time a maniac tried to take over everything. That was a long game too and cost millions of lives before victory came, finally, six years later. Back then, it was a human war with human limitations on advancements and further plots. Now, this was something else. This was human versus superhuman and, it seemed, the latter had no limitation.

Patience was all he had but patience for what? A soft landing? Some magic moment where the madness suddenly stopped and all was well? Redsaw just simply vanishing along with those who worked for him?

For a moment, Jack thought of Axiom-man again. Maybe with him, there might have been a chance.

But Axiom-man was dead . . .

. . . and soon the city would be too.

Battle Bruiser dangled his arm out of the window of the cab of the large semi, engine running. On the trailer bed sat the metal tubs from the roof of Owen Tower, each one filled with silver bars. They were stacked and strapped down.

"Thi . . . be . . . lo . . . fly," Lady Fire said near the front of the engine.

"What?" Bruiser said. "Ya gotta speak up, Lady."

She turned and faced him. "I said this going to be a long flight!"

Her voice barely made over the rumble of the engine but he heard her. "Yeah, well, hopefully it'll only be one of one . . . unless you plan on coming back."

She crossed her arms. "Right now, it's not what I want. It's what he wants. Let's just get this done and see what our options are."

"Right." He glanced back at the metal molding tubs then set his face to the windshield. "Let's get this going." He put the truck in gear and started the roll forward. Lady Fire would stay ahead of him to guard the truck. "Flin Flon. Stupid name." It was an old mining town up north surrounded by rocky hills. Why Redsaw chose the location, he didn't know. All he was told to do was take the molds up north. Though Bruiser knew Redsaw could have flown them up there himself, he suspected there was unfinished business here hence the stay-back. Besides, who was he to question Redsaw when the man could destroy him with a single blast?

"Whatever, whatever, whatever," he said and pressed on the gas.

It was going to be a long ride.

———

The call went out to Charlie's associates. Many were scattered throughout the city so it would take some time to bring everyone in.

Charlie sat at his desk, drumming his fingers against the table. *What is he planning?* His mind flicked over to the image of a large crowd of people—his people—standing before Redsaw, ready to receive orders. "Whatever he's planning, it's big." He took a drag off his cigar. "Real big." He knew with how things have gone so far that as long as you played by Redsaw's rules, you were okay. To be fair, Charlie had little to complain about other than being under orders from someone else. The job was lucrative, his men seldom getting hurt unless they crossed the line with someone from another gang and, even then, getting hurt wasn't always guaranteed.

But, he had to admit, it did feel good to be feel invincible. He barely ever walked the street alone but when he did, folks knew who he was and side-stepped out of his way, giving him a worried look. To a degree, he felt like a fool for not doing what Redsaw had done almost right from the get-go: Plow in by force and take what you needed. At the same time, such an effort would've been met by the cops, Axiom-man, and anyone else with the means to shut down their operation. As much as a gun held a lot of power, it was no match for someone with even better firepower, including people like the cops and armed forces. Everything had to be done under the table to avoid most issues. Lots of secrets. Lots of hidden methods of transporting illicit goods from one end of the city to the other with equally secret methods of laundering the money so it came out clean on the other side.

Charlie knew better than to question if Redsaw knew what he was doing. The man wasn't relying purely on his strength and power to get things done. There was obviously a very sharp mind behind that cowl deciding what string to pull and when.

"Everybody in," he said and took another puff off his cigar.

———

"Dude, this is crazy," Smokejob said. "Smokejob" was Robbie's nickname because he always had a cigarette dangling out of his mouth. He swung his head left then right, eyes wide with paranoia.

"I don't care," Deck said. "Deck" was short for Deacon. "Look, I need some air."

"This is not air, man. This is walking around the aftermath of a forest fire."

"You know what I mean."

Smokejob sighed and ran his hand over his tight, curly hair. "Couldn't you have just stuck your head out the window?"

Deck gave him a wry look . . . then tears glazed over his eyes. "Vanessa was everything and . . . and she got gunned down over a dumb bag of groceries. Gunned. Down."

Smokejob set the jokes aside. He knew Deck was hurting and had grown more reckless since two and half weeks ago when Vanessa was killed. He couldn't blame the guy. Out of everyone in the group, Deck was the romantic, and when he met Vanessa, that was it. Romanticism locked, loaded, and ready for life, and, it seemed, Vanessa was on board with that, too. The two of them were hardly seen one without the other. It was almost like watching a set of clones but opposite genders, they had so much in common.

"Sorry, man," Smokejob said. "I know she was a big deal."

Deck gave him a shove against the wall they walked by. Smokejob bumped into it. Hitting the wall didn't hurt but the shove was fairly pointed. "Not just a big deal. *The* deal. Show some respect."

"Sorry." Smokejob straightened himself and continued walking.

Deck had his hands in his pockets, his face pointed this way and that as if exploring the streets the two of them had walked many times before. "You know, sometimes I wonder if I got hit in the head and this"

—he gestured around them— "is all some sort of weird mix in my head—probably my multitude of issues—and when I wake up, I get to roll over and see her."

Smokejob didn't answer. He'd heard this little speech before. It was Deck's go-to. Maybe because a dream—nightmare—was still better than real life these days. Unfortunately, Smokejob never found that girl, *his* girl. He'd loved before, but with the way Deck was head-over-heels nuts for Vanessa made him wonder if he'd ever experienced the real thing at all. It didn't really matter now. Not with the city the way it was. Not with anything the way it was.

The second Smokejob set his foot down on the pavement at the mouth of an alley, what felt like a small car plowed into both him and Deck and sent them into the dark. The two were on the ground in no time.

Smokejob rolled onto his back and looked up. The only light was from the mouth of the alley and even that was dim. He couldn't make out any faces but there were at least six guys standing over the two of them, one significantly larger than the others. Probably the same dude who ran into them and sent them hurtling into the alley.

"Quick. Simple. Done," one of the guys said. "Anything you got on you, I don't care what it is. Just make sure it's something I can sell."

Smokejob looked over to Deck, who was only now seeming to assemble himself and was on his back too. He tried to sit up but a boot to his chest sent him back down.

"I said quick, simple, done. Don't make 'done' your face smashed in never mind involuntary castration."

Deck shot Smokejob a dose of wide-eyed panic.

"It's okay," Smokejob said quietly. "Just give them what they want. What do ya got on ya?"

"Nothing," Deck said. "I know the rules."

"Rules?"

"Leave your stuff at home."

"That's not a—" A thud ran through Smokejob's head and it wasn't until a few seconds later when the pain kicked in did he realize he got another boot. He kept his head as flat as possible against the pavement to avoid another.

"Search them," the seeming leader of the pack said.

Within half a moment, hands were all over Smokejob's body. A part of him wanted to make some sort of smartass remark but he knew that if he opened his trap, it'd get quickly closed.

He stole a glance in Deck's direction. Two guys had their hands in every pocket Deck had on his person, his heart-broken friend lying there frozen, arms out as if being searched at the airport.

Deck got a punch to the face but it didn't send him under.

"Nothing," one of the guys said.

Smokejob really wished he could see their faces or even a clearer outline of their bodies, but it was too dark. Just rimmed shadows.

One of the shadows ripped a plastic card out of Smokejob's front pants pocket. "What's this? Credit?"

Smokejob spat out a touch of blood. "A Tim Horton's points card."

There was a pause. "You got to be kidding me. No credit?"

The credit card machines aren't working anyway, you dumb idiot. "No." Another boot to the face and this one sent Smokejob reeling. His head torqued to the right, cheek pressed against the pavement. While the dull pain rocked his head and the sting of the bottom of the boot rested on his left cheek, he knew the next thing to come would be a stomping and, worse, it would literally be that. The shadows would team up and then plow their feet down upon him and his friend as if destroying grapes in an old wine press.

"P-please," Deck said. His voice was barely a whisper and had a lisp to it. Maybe one of his teeth got knocked out?

"Quick, simple, done," the guy said.

Smokejob squeezed his eyes shut, braced himself, and tried to get his arms up in front of his face like a shield. The boot came down but seemed to almost springboard off his arms, touching and then bouncing off. He opened his eyes and the shadows remained above him but . . . at least one less, maybe two. It was hard to tell in the dark.

Where?

"Guys," one of the shadows said. "Guys?"

Smokejob was sure he'd been struck but maybe struck so hard it was taking a while for his nerves to come around and send the pain signals to his brain. It seemed like there were less shadows over him. Had they moved over to Deck?

Deck!

Smokejob glanced over. His buddy lay on the ground in a similar posture, arms curled up around his head. Smokejob couldn't tell if Deck could see anything at all.

A shadow loomed over Deck and Smokejob each . . . then seemed to get sucked over to the shadows of the alley on the sides.

"What?" Smokejob started.

"Vanessa, Vanessa, Vanessa," Deck whispered. "Gonna see you soon. Gonna see you soon. Gonna see you—"

"Deck," Smokejob whispered.

"—soon. Gonna—"

"Deck!"

"—see . . . . What?" A few seconds later he slowly pulled his arms from off his face.

Strangely, it was only now the panic truly set in and Smokejob found himself breathing heavy. "They're . . . they're . . . gone."

"What?"

Smokejob reached a hand over onto Deck's shoulder. "Hang on. Don't move. Just in case."

There had been no sound. Just darkness swallowing darkness, shadows removed.

"Slowly," Deck said.

Carefully, the two sat upright. Smokejob scanned the alley as best as he could given the light and couldn't see nor hear those guys anywhere. "I think we're alone."

Deck caught his breath. When he spoke, his words were thick and partially coherent, evidence of two fat lips. "Alone."

Chapter Five

FLIN FLON'S POPULATION had doubled since Redsaw took his position in the city, many folks fleeing up north for refuge. It was all done discreetly and Redsaw scolded himself for not taking notice. No one had said there had been an exodus. Though a departure was expected, most of it was contained by him using his red energy to blow a massive hole in all highways leading out of the city. Redsaw had been thorough as well. Maps were employed and even some old roads that could achieve an exit were destroyed. Still, it seemed, some folks took a chance with their vehicles and worked around the problem over uneven terrain.

No matter. Whether they were here or up north, this province was his and Battle Bruiser was in the midst of his part of getting that done.

There was a rap on the roof's door while Redsaw stood at the foot of the stairs leading up to his throne. "Enter."

A man came through, a nice, dark pin-striped suit with Spatz polished to a shine. "Um, sir?"

"I know who you are, Tony."

"You do?"

"I make it my business to know. What do you want?"

"You know me?"

Redsaw glared at him.

"Um, just a report from Charlie. Most of his boys are gathered, some still coming in. He said the other leaders are roughly in the same position. He . . . he wanted to pass on an update."

"And he didn't tell me this himself, why?"

"Busy, sir, but he told me to make it clear it wasn't a case of being too busy for *you*. Just busy making sure all is in order as you asked."

It was an acceptable answer, but Redsaw held Tony's gaze anyway, an intimidating affirmation of who was really in control. After a long minute, Redsaw turned. "Good. Go."

From behind him, "Yes, sir." A moment after, the roof door closed.

"Conglomeration," Redsaw said and ascended the steps.

———

The room glowed bright reds and oranges as Cicilia backed herself into the corner of the room, the only place not yet scorched by the flames. Smoke clouded the air in full except for about six inches off the burning floor where it was slightly thinner.

Cicilia watched in horror as gray and black smoke billowed out her apartment window, her couch, TV, desk—everything else aflame and blocking any chance of an exit. She didn't know who had it in for her when the Molotov cocktail crashed through her window. The moment the bottle burst open against the wall, everything lit up. Before she had a chance to get to the door, the plastic in the carpet went up like kindling, disabling her from leaving lest she run through the flames. She had thought about it but the flames had run so close to the door she'd have to stand in the fire to unlock everything then get out. And despite a moment of being willing to take the risk, it was foiled when the wooden door caught fire as well.

Now, in the corner, flames creeping up on her, Cicilia made the Sign of the Cross and began quickly uttering prayers in Spanish as tears rolled down her cheeks.

The heat of the flames pressed in and despite her mouth barely opening for her words, sharp, foul smoke still made its way into her mouth and nostrils, causing her to cough and gag.

"Padre!" she cried heavenward.

The flames licked her long T-shirt; she batted out the ones that sent the edges of her garment on fire.

Tears in full force now, heart pounding harder than ever, she was convinced she was having a heart attack. She debated if she should just dive into the flames and get it over with or await the slow burn.

"O Padre, O Padre, O Padre . . ." She hoped God heard her otherwise she'd be seeing Him soon anyway.

She squeezed her eyes shut and braced for the searing and sizzling heat of the fire to touch her skin before engulfing her in full.

All she could do was weep.

The heat grew and her skin began to sting as its temperature quickly rose. She couldn't watch. Couldn't look. Coughed. Gagged. Spat. Eyes now squeezed shut as the sharp smoke stung her eyeballs and made her cry.

Any moment now and her nerve endings would be seared. For a split second she thought maybe she wouldn't feel the flames and her own self-cooking if that happened.

The heat.

Too much.

She cried out a blather of sound and tears.

"Padre," she whispered, the tears so much they rolled down her lips like drool.

All was dark when something firm grabbed each of her shoulders. Cicilia tried to look to see what it was but couldn't open her eyes because of the smoke. Coughing and wheezing, she let the grip upon her take her. A quick bump to the stomach indicated she had just been bent over some thing, no wider than half a foot, maybe a bit more. She coughed and spat and cried.

A quick flash of heat then a sudden acceleration and burst of cold air . . . then nothing but falling.

Still bent over and hoarsely screaming, Cicilia squeezed her eyes open and closed as fast and as best as able, allowing the tears to help clear the dark a little. Everything was ablur, pavement rushing up to meet her. Had she jumped out the window out of instinct and now would die by splattering all over the ground? What about the fact she was bent in half in an upside-down U over something. She tried to take a look at what had her but saw nothing and only heard a long, soft buzzing sound as if an extremely long zipper was being undone. Her descent slowed until speed was no longer a factor.

Cicilia hit the ground with her hip but the impact was mild. By the time she cleared the tears from her eyes and coughed out the smoke, there was only wonder.

She was on the street safely away from the burning floor of her building.

There was no one around.

Battle Bruiser didn't mind driving at night. In the old days, that meant fewer cars on the road, quieter and less stimulation on the eyes thanks to the darkness, the only light being the high beams. It was his own place of serenity.

But not tonight. The cargo in the back was critical and he didn't want to know what Redsaw would do to him if he didn't make the delivery on time.

"No issues," Redsaw had told him. "Understood?"

"Yes, sir."

He crept up on the town and kept his eyes toward the sky. Other than the moon being a haze behind some thin clouds, the sky was barren. But, not for long.

"Ah, there you are, my dear," Battle Bruiser said when he spotted Lady Fire light up her flames in the sky. "Make your point, my lady. Let them know I'm coming."

Lady Fire hovered in the sky. Any moment now and she'd herald Battle Bruiser's arrival.

"Come on, come on, you can do it," he said.

About half a minute passed then Lady Fire lit up her hands and blasted the ground with as much flame as she could throw, spreading her fire around as if spraying a hose to clean off a messy spill. Her flames hit the ground with such force chunks of dirt and rock spewed upward in a glorious rain of chaos.

Battle Bruiser drove through the falling debris, past Lady Fire, and entered the town. It wasn't long past eleven at night so some folks were still up. Those that were peered out their windows or came out of their doors to see what was going on. For his own amusement, Battle Bruiser offered a nonchalant wave as he drove past them as if he was a milkman.

"Er, too bad this thing don't have no ice cream tunes. Would've been hilarious." He barked out a laugh and kept going.

The first target: the highest rocky hill in town.

It was time to show the residents that fleeing was a bad idea.

NEW DAWN

A small parade of Infinitys, Mercedes, Porches, and one Lamborghini drove down Portage Avenue.

One destination: Redsaw's throne.

Margaret sat on her sofa, her head on her arm, fast asleep. The only light was the lamp on the small corner table beside the couch. The fatigue wasn't because of the hour; it was because she hadn't eaten in three days. Fortunately, she still had water, but that could only fill the stomach so much. At least the water kept her alive, but she lost count of how many times she spewed it up because of nausea from being so hungry. Getting food was growing harder by the day. For the first part of Redsaw's reign, the food delivery system that had always been in place functioned more or less normally, but once he took hold of the food supply, whatever consumable items that were left in the city were hunted down, raided in full, with nothing left for anyone else. She wasn't sure if his endgame was to kill everybody through starvation or feed them just enough so they wouldn't die but would be too weak for much of a resistance.

As if resistance was even possible at this point anyway.

Despite three deadbolts, a standard knob lock, and a chain, her door blasted open when five men slammed through with a battering ram. Before she could think of how they got through in one blow, they filled her apartment, with two heading right for her. All she acknowledged about the other three before she was grabbed off the couch was they headed further into her apartment and, from the sound, started knocking things over and digging around.

One dark-haired man in a black sweatsuit and a gaze that seemed to be operating off pure instinct stood directly in front of her, his hands pinning her wrists to the sides of her thighs, forcing her to face him. The other man was behind her and had a hand just below each of her shoulders. Margaret tried to twist and squirm her way out but the grip was like a vice, and after her fourth twist, she got a hard open hand to her cheek. Tears immediately blurred her vision.

"Front or back," the man in front of her said to the man behind.

"You know me," the other man replied. Margaret hadn't got a good look at him but judging by the tone of his voice, she knew he was about to say, "Any side is fine."

He said it.

The man behind her pulled her onto him so both landed on the couch, the man in front with one hand raised as if to strike, the other fumbling with his pants.

More tears blossomed and ran down her face and dribbled off her lip. "No no no, please."

"Yes yes yes, please," he replied.

She tried to swing at him but her arms got nowhere, held back good and sure. She attempted a feeble kick from her sitting position but that was quickly swatted away as the man in front drew closer.

"Don't fight," he said, "or we fight back."

"You . . . can't," she said. "How could . . . you?" The tears streamed and all she could do was fall crushed beneath the weight of what was about to happen. *Just go inside, just go inside. Let the outside go. Be inside.* But the consciousness separation attempt was immediately shut down by the fear of not knowing how long it would go on.

"One for the money," the man said.

"Two for the show," the man she sat on said.

"No . . . don't. Please. Please please please."

"I like begging," the man said. "But I want the right kind." He gave her a knowing look.

It all fell apart and she let out a wail as he put his body against hers. Howling cries poured from her mouth and she began to gag from the sudden exertion.

The lights went out.

Completely.

The man in front of her disappeared into darkness. The two men were still there because they still held her. Beyond, elsewhere in the apartment, she heard, "What the hell?" and "Hey!"

Slow footsteps in the other rooms. For a quick moment, the image of the others trying to find their way in the dark crossed her mind. She was abruptly brought back to the men who had her tightened in their vice.

Then release.

The weighted pressure of the man in front ceased and something yanked her from the other man and sent her off to the side. She stumbled a few steps to the side before hitting the wall. She slid down it, using it as an anchor point in the dark.

She didn't hear anything besides the one-by-one thud of what sounded like bodies hitting her apartment floor.

Margaret dug her hand in her pocket, felt around, then pulled out her lighter. She flicked the flint and shone the little flame at her living room.

All five men were piled up in the middle, each unconscious, each leaking blood from their mouths and noses, the faces she could see sporting the beginning swells of two black eyes.

A whisper: "Leave."

"Who are you? Who's there?" she yelled.

There was no reply.

The men remained silent in their heap.

CHAPTER SIX

THE MIX OF black and gray clouds that covered the city ensured it remained in perpetual night. Clouds from the Doorway spilled out and billowed into the sky, mixing with the natural clouds above, the cloud so think it blocked out the sun and transformed it into a faded moon.

"Let me do it," she said.

"No, I can do it," he replied.

"You can't. Not yet. If word gets out . . ."

"I see your point."

Below, Dave's Bar's neon sign flickered as it struggled to retain whatever electricity was flowing into it.

"You can't go in," he said.

"I'm not."

Dave's sign was quickly covered as gray fabric sprung out to the left and right over it. The fabric descended and the neon sign was back in view.

———

Dave's Bar was where it started for Night Fowler, for Katie. It was here she met "Mike" and soon found herself on a new path in her private pursuit of justice.

Meeting Mike changed everything. Perhaps, without him, she wouldn't be Night Fowler today.

Her boots hit the street and she let her cape close in around her like a second skin.

It was 7:06AM. At 7:10, Jimmy Timmy would stumble out of the bar for a leak like he always did. Why he didn't use the facilities inside was anyone's guess, but what

Jimmy lacked in a confident-sounding nickname, he certainly made up for by being a man of information, drunk or not.

Night Fowler glanced up at the rooftop she came from. The ledge was vacant. Good.

The clock ticked a slow four minutes, but sure enough, Jimmy stepped into the back alley right on time.

Remaining out of view, Night Fowler eyed him as he made his way to the back corner where Dave's Bar backed up against another building in the Exchange District. Even from here, she heard his zipper go down. Another second and he'd be very vulnerable.

While Jimmy painted the wall with his own special signature, she approached and soon had him in a rear-naked choke, cutting off any verbal reaction.

Jimmy batted at the forearm clamped under his chin in a feeble attempt for release.

Night Fowler made sure he didn't see her face. "Now, now, Jimmy, move anymore and you might lose it."

Jimmy dipped his head slightly forward with the minimal movement he had as if checking to make sure all was still intact. He moved to zip up but Night Fowler spun him around then sent his face back against the brick wall.

"Don't. Touch," she said.

Jimmy slowly raised his hands in surrender as she tightened the noose and stopped the air from entering his lungs for a solid ten seconds. When she released enough so he could gulp some oxygen, nothing but gagging followed. She tightened up on his neck again, shutting him up.

"Come on, Jimmy, I thought you were tougher than that? Aren't you also known as 'The Safe'? Someone puts in a file and you're invincible for retrieval after?"

He began to slump in her arms. She let up and all that entered his lungs were wheezing breaths. She abruptly turned him around, gave him a slap, then turned him back around again. A moment later, a foggy Jimmy returned.

"Wha—what do . . . you want?" he said.

"Open the Safe."

"Never."

Night Fowler adjusted her arm and got her thumb and index finger clamped around his trachea from behind. Jimmy jolted forward as it was slowly crushed. Feebly, he waved his hands in the air, a clear indicator he wanted her to stop.

"Open it," she said.

He waved both palms at the wrist, the palms doing the nodding for him.

She let go.

Jimmy tried to turn around but she kept him facing the wall. With a quick double strike, she sent a muscle spasm through both his shoulders, making it difficult for him to have the strength to lift his arms for the next little while. She sent a knee into the back of his, folding it and forcing him to kneel.

"Safe," she said.

"If I give you the key, I'm a dead man."

"Spare the metaphors."

"You started it."

She brought a hammer fist down on the top of his head, forcing his neck into a momentary suppression. All he could produce was a low "oof" with the minimal air that was no doubt in his lungs.

"The Safe is empty, at least, in terms of what you're looking for, and I know what you're looking for. You a cop?"

She sent him under with one strike to the base of the skull.

———

Bruiser grunted as he hauled the tubs of silver up to the highest rocky point in Flin Flon. As much as Lady Fire was a help in keeping the townspeople under submission, she was useless in the muscle department.

At the top of the hill, he plunked the tub down, removed his hat, and wiped the sweat off his forehead. Big strength, sure, but big endurance, not so much.

He had an idea. He put his hat back on then stuffed the tips of two fingers into his mouth and shrieked a whistle. Lady Fire turned in the air in his direction.

"Blast the rock," he shouted. "Carve me a path."

"Why?"

"Just do it!"

Fire poured from her hands. The speeding impact of the flames didn't damage the rocks but they began to heat. Any and all inherent metals within the rock of this mining town would melt and, eventually, begin to flow.

Battle Bruiser needed a straight path to finish this.

———

When Jimmy came to, he was strung up by the wrists and hanging from a fire escape rail. Night Fowler remained on the platform behind him.

"Now are we ready to talk?" she asked.

Jimmy glanced down. Though only about twenty feet above street level, to him it must have looked like a hundred because he screamed . . . then was silenced when a thick glove wrapped itself around his mouth.

"The Safe," she said.

He nodded. She removed her hand. "It's pretty bare. Has been since . . . he . . . took over. Information is tight. No one talks. All are afraid. One guy got popped just for mentioning you-know-who's name, and another got sliced to ribbons because he shared a rumor that wasn't true."

"And?"

"I've got nothing, you . . . you . . . whoever you are."

"I don't believe you."

He sighed. "Cut me down."

"Gladly . . . but then you'll fall and break your legs. Want that?"

Jimmy appeared to think about it. He glanced down and she knew he noticed she hadn't zipped him up. "Oh come on. I'm hanging here with my d—"

"Now, now, let's use nice words, Jimmy. Spill it or I drop you."

"And if I have nothing like I said?"

"I'll drop you anyway."

He let out a small cough, turned his head left to right then looked back down. "I swear this is the truth. Please, you have to believe me. This is all I got."

"What?"

"Movement. That's all I know. Things are shuffling. People are moving. Some guys . . . . Let me go!" He twisted in the air as if trying to loose the bonds. It took a moment but he settled. "Some guys . . . *the* guys . . . haven't been seen in days. Top brass."

"Who?"

"All of them."

She grabbed him by the hair and jerked his head around every which way to induce disorientation. "Keep being vague," she said as she moved his head around, "and soon you'll be hanging with forty-proof puke all over you."

"Stooop."

She kept it up a moment longer then relented. "Who!"

"I don't have names. No such thing. Not anymore. Anyone who runs an area has multiple names so nobody knows who's talking about who unless you know the chain."

"Chain?"

"Of name flow. You know, Bob turns into Sam who turns into Tom who—"

"What is he . . . she . . . them called right now?"

"I don't know. I lost the chain. Sorry."

"Don't make me make you mean that word."

"I told you all I got in the Safe. Top brass, all gone, along with most under them. Where or when, I don't know. Truth, I swear. The past couple of years have created some underground info chain I can't follow. I'm good, but not that good."

"Maybe you should be," she said. She put two fingers to the side of his neck to check his pulse. It raced, which was expected. The main thing was checking his eyes, face. There were no giveaways here for a lie.

Night Fowler reached for a pouch on her belt, pulled out a line and knife, then connected the line to his bonds. "Thanks for the info. If I find out you're lying" —she glanced down between his legs— "you're going to lose it." In one fluid motion, she cut his bonds from the rail and used the line to drop him to the ground. She made sure gravity was enough to make his legs fold on impact but not break anything.

Jimmy merely lay in the alleyway behind Dave's Bar below, curled up like a child.

———

"Are you sure he doesn't know anything?" he asked.

"I'm sure," Night Fowler said with assurance, eyes still on Jimmy below. "We need information and only so much can be obtained through observance."

"Observance is the starting point."

"Always is." She turned and faced Axiom-man.

She was stoic, which was who Katie was when in her uniform. Axiom-man admired that about her, the calm. He knew that, right now, as she looked at him, all she saw was a figure mostly in shadow. His new uniform was the same design as his previous one but without a cape and his hair was covered. What was light blue fabric was now dark gray and what was dark blue was now black. Even his golden belt buckle was displayed as dirty, brushed nickel. This belt was different, however, for it held weapons and tools for their mission. Little items Night Fowler gave him a crash course on to help with their mission. Things like explosives.

"You all right being back?" she asked.

"Yes . . . and no," he said. He took a breath and slowly let it out. "It's good to be back home but my heart aches over what it's become." He glanced at the surrounding buildings, most with broken windows and a few with chunks of its construction missing. "It's also a reminder of her."

Night Fowler remained silent.

"But it doesn't matter," he said. "We need to fix this."

"You cannot activate your powers," she said.

"Stop. You've told me that precisely seven times already. I know the reason." Why she kept on him about it, he didn't know. Was there a temptation he wasn't seeing? After all, Night Fowler was better trained than he was. At some point, did he give away the idea he would turn them on? "I will remain in the dark. He can't sense I'm here. Now stop. No more reminders."

She eyed him then finally nodded.

"Was Jimmy our only source?" he asked.

"The only source with what we would have needed to know."

Axiom-man took a moment to accept the words. They needed intel and clearly Redsaw was keeping a lid on his plans so they didn't make their way to gossip on the street.

"We need someone to talk to," she said.

Axiom-man looked to the left. Over there was an option. "I can only think of one person." *If he's still alive.*

Chapter Seven

Jack Gunn rolled out of bed and almost hit the floor upon standing, his head swooned so much. He glanced at the bourbon bottle on the night table beside his bed. It was maybe an inch full but definitely not more than that. Right now, the very sight of the bottle—he had to look away lest he risk throwing up.

Too late.

He felt the contents of his gut rise to the surface and he debated if it was best to swallow it down or let it come out. Head aching with emphasis of a sharp pain around his eye sockets, he was in no mood to let it all out so he swallowed. At first, it was okay . . . then his stomach did a flip and kicked everything back up to the surface. Partially-digested food and a whole lot of half-processed alcohol burst out of his mouth and splashed onto the floor.

Crap! Crapcrapcrap! He let the moment run its course, spat, then waited hunched over until the wave of nausea passed. When he straightened himself, his stomach felt a lot better but everything was a haze as if he was looking *at* his life instead of being *in* it.

He put a palm by his eyes, forbidding his sight to see the bottle on the table. He pressed a hand over his forehead. "You're an idiot," he muttered then slowly made his way to the bathroom. Once done, Jack headed to the kitchen, hoping there was Ginger Ale or 7-Up in the fridge. He grimaced when he opened the door and found the shelves near bare and without the pop he was looking for.

"Yep," was all he said then reached for a glass from the cupboard. He took the glass to the sink and filled it to the brim. He drank slowly, not wanting to trigger another stomach upset by gulping it down despite being so thirsty. Once done, he refilled the glass halfway, finished that, then set the glass down. He waited a moment to make sure his stomach was calm before heading to the living room, feet dragging along the carpet. "Don't know what I'm doing." Why the living room and not back to bed, he didn't know other than he didn't want to sleep. Before, sleep and dreams were a pleasant escape from reality. Over the past two years, those dreams had turned into nightmares and the majority of them contained different elements of what was going on outside his window.

Jack slumped in his easy chair and closed his eyes. When he opened them, he reached for the switch on the lamp beside him. The light didn't go on. "What the—?" He tried again. And again. Nothing. "Burnt out?" He fumbled to locate the lightbulb in the dark. Though he wouldn't be able to see the scorch mark from a burnt-out bulb, he'd still be able to hear the filament rattling around inside the bulb if he removed it from the lamp and gave it a shake to confirm it was of no more use.

Except . . . the bulb was missing. Did he already know it was burnt out, meant to change it, got as far as removing the bulb but then got distracted by the booze and forgot all about it? No. Booze affected his judgement like everyone else but after years on the force, he understood the importance of concentrating through a fuzzy head and, over time, made it a subconscious habit.

"Fine," he said and set his palms on the armrests. The intent was to get up, go to the hallway closet and see if he had extra bulbs in there. The second he put his weight on his palms to get up, something gripped his arms from both sides and yanked him back down into his seat. The shock of the unexpected touch made him bolt upright only to be pulled back down again. This time, the moment he was plunked back in the chair, a gloved hand covered his mouth.

"Don't talk," a voice whispered.

Jack turned partway around in his chair to take a swipe at whoever was in his apartment but was quickly spun back facing forward, hand still over his mouth, something dull pressing into the soft underside of his jawbone. He squealed from the pain and the hand pressed against his mouth harder.

"Don't move," the whisper said again.

Though the words were muffled and hardly understandable, Jack said, "What . . . do . . . you want?"

"Help."

"With . . . what?"

"Redsaw."

The moment the name was spoken, a hollow pang hit Jack's heart as his stomach sank. The pressure of the hand against his mouth began to slowly release. All Jack said was, "There is no help for that."

The hand released. A shadow emerged beside him, making its way to the front of the chair. Jack got himself ready to lunge at the invader.

The shadow spoke loud and clear, "Don't be so sure, Jack."

Wait. What? No. "Axiom-man?"

Axiom-man stood before Jack, the room dark, Gunn's features barely visible in the shadows. "It's been a long time, Jack."

"You're . . . you're . . . supposed to be dead." Gunn put his face in his hands. Axiom-man could smell the booze on him. "Another nightmare. Great."

Axiom-man tossed the light bulb onto Jack's lap. "Do nightmares do that?"

"Only the ones that want you to think they're real."

"Always an answer for everything. Good to see you, Jack."

It was then it seemed to click for Gunn he wasn't dreaming. He picked up the bulb and rolled it around in his palm. "Turn the light on."

"No."

"You giving me orders?"

"Yes." Jack rolled the bulb around in his hand for a few more seconds then set it beside the base of the lamp. He took a breath before speaking. "Where have you been?"

"Away."

"I know that. Why?"

"Had to be done."

"So we're on short answers now, huh? Well, good enough." He looked in Axiom-man's direction but judging by the way his eyes were moving, he couldn't get a lock on him in the shadows.

"Is your head on straight enough to talk?"

"Is my head . . . . Look, you're the one with his head on crooked, as always." It seemed Jack was finally caught up, acting like his usual jerkish self. "If you are who you say you are, you're an idiot. No, an idiot times ten. Eleven. Friggin' a hundred!" He nodded toward him. "Show me."

"What?"

"Some blue light. Prove it."

"No."

"Then you could be anybody. Get outta here before I shoot you."

Axiom-man grabbed Gunn by the arm, hoisted him out of the chair and onto his feet, then immediately put the man's arm into a chicken wing behind his back, one hand maintaining the arm lock, the other grabbing Jack by the hair on the back of his head.

"Hey!" Jack struggled against the hold. Axiom-man increased the pressure on his arm, forcing him to stop.

"Do you want it broken?"

"You're not him. He was never this violent."

"This isn't violent, Jack." He jerked up Jack's arm further, making the man howl. Axiom-man pulled his head back by the hair, stopping him. "Violence is reserved for those who need to be brought to justice. For you? This is me reacting to your reaction." Axiom-man let Jack's head straighten.

"Always an answer," Jack said, his tone indicating he believed him.

Axiom-man kept the heat on his arm and head and shoved Jack toward the window then pressed Gunn's face against the glass. "See that?"

"Let. Go."

"You let the city crumble. You let people die."

"Can . . . you . . . ease . . . off?"

Axiom-man let go of his head, giving him enough room to properly look out the window.

"The . . . arm."

Axiom-man didn't release the hold. "Your job was to go after enhanced humans and bring them in. You didn't." He slammed Jack back up against the window. "Why?"

"Because . . . because you were gone."

Axiom-man pulled him back from the window a few inches. "That's irrelevant. You had a job to do and you didn't do it."

"You're not the same guy, are ya?" Gunn said. "The voice is the same but he never acted this way."

"New game. New rules."

"I ain't playing."

Axiom-man released his arm, spun Jack around, then sent him to the ground with a push kick. "Tell me."

Gunn hit the ground with a thud. "What?"

Axiom-man remained silent. It seemed as if Gunn was still toying with the idea of an attack.

"Look, I'll keep it simple. The roof got blown off Owen Tower, you . . . or him . . . went missing and Redsaw made himself overlord of the entire city. My taskforce *and* job were terminated and now the place is run by mob bosses and people in tights. The city is cut off at all entry points plus a few other barriers. No one in or out."

"Law enforcement?"

"Gone. I mean, some guys help out now and then if they stumble across an incident that won't get them killed, but everyone went home to their families or pets or to the bottle. Rumor has it several went home with their gun and never came back out the door."

"Military?"

"Not allowed in. That shmuck made sure of that. The second the jeeps and tanks rolled into town, Redsaw made short work of them then kept a few alive and did a little demo on a few civilians on what would happen to anyone who interfered. It was disgusting. He held those people high up, his hand acting like a noose, and then just fried them to a crisp." Jack ran a hand down his face. "I don't know. There was a second attempt from the outside and that time Redsaw destroyed the vehicles but made sure their destruction lasted long enough for him to stand on the hood of the vehicle as those trapped inside watched him watch them burn alive."

"And?"

"There were rumors of an airstrike but nothing was dropped or sent our way. Either whoever was in charge changed their mind or Redsaw took them out in the air. Regardless, there is no outside help and those here on the inside are too scared to do anything but comply."

"Where is he now?"

"Probably on that rooftop of his. Spends a lot of time up there. Only comes out for . . . special occasions."

"Special occasions?"

Jack looked up at him. "Murder."

Axiom-man's heart normally would have sank at the news but after spending all that time training with Aiyesha, he was taught to keep his emotions at bay during a crisis and then to deal with them later.

"Jack, listen to me," Axiom-man said.

Gunn looked his way.

"I wasn't here. You got up, made a mess of yourself, then cleaned up and went back to bed. Understood?"

"Understood," Jack whispered.

"I'll be in touch."

CHAPTER EIGHT

"OH LOOK AT my big, strong man carrying so much weight," Lady Fire said as Battle Bruiser towed via rope a silver tub along the cooled path up the hill. She made sure she added a little *I Love Lucy* to her tone.

"Quiet, ya insect," Bruiser said, grunting his way up the incline.

"Why not drive them up?"

"Because the truck would be back-heavy and the ground ain't good enough for traction. The truck tips and guess who goes rolling back with it?"

"So?"

"So? We only have one truck! Besides, I'm not going to make a mess of things for yer amusement."

She stuck out her bottom lip in a pout. "Oh darn. And here I was thinking I was with a man who knew what he was doing."

"That's what women think," he muttered.

"I heard that."

"Heh."

Bruiser continued towing the rope secured to the tub of silver up the hill.

"Gonna set up as you go along or . . . ?"

"Mission one is get these suckers to the top. Mission two is a break."

"Mission three?"

"I only do two missions at a time."

———

The warehouse was near the perimeter that bordered the city, an oval stretch of highway that wrapped itself around Winnipeg so you could exit the city, circle to where you wanted, then enter back in and save driving time. Out here . . . no one had been out here in a long time. The place was an old, heavy-duty parts factory. Metal beams and thick chains were the décor along with abandoned welding tools, pressing machines, stand-up drills, and various devices used for molding and shaping metal.

Now, at night, the place would have been pitch black if not for the slew of high-beam flashlights that some of the men carried, illuminating the place enough to see everyone.

Over six hundred men and women crowded the floor of the factory. What could be pushed aside was pushed aside. Tables and stations that were bolted down were used for leaning or sitting. Surrounding the inner perimeter of the warehouse above was a catwalk with access ladders on all four sides of the building.

For Charlie, the climb to the top of the catwalk was a climb of victory and symbolic of his ascension amongst Redsaw's ranks. But deep down he knew there was no ascending. Not in the way he hoped, but it didn't matter. If Redsaw's plan came to fruition, there'd be plenty to go around for everybody.

Charlie reached the catwalk, sturdied his feet under him, tugged on his overcoat to straighten it, then proceeded to the center where all could see him.

Once there, he merely stood, not moving nor speaking, and waited. Below, the eyes that caught sight of him turned in his direction to face him. Soon, others noticed people looking so followed suit. Within a few minutes, all eyes were on him.

He waited a moment longer, face stoic, hands folded in front of his thighs. Then, "Good evening, ladies and gentlemen. Thank you for coming out to this place."

"Nice and convenient," someone muttered below.

"Yes, nice and convenient," Charlie said, "which it is. We are here undisturbed and unnoticed." He paused. "I know some of you have come—relatively speaking—far, your domain well on the other end of where we now stand. Note that every one of you is appreciated for coming. Does anybody notice anyone missing?"

Folks turned their heads left and right. No one spoke.

"No matter. Whomever couldn't make it can be filled in. Ain't a great thing either, so that's on you, by the way." He unfolded his hands then took hold of each of his coat's lapels. "Tonight I have an announcement."

Any remaining whispers and murmurs silenced.

"You are free," he said. "Free to roam and do as you please. Some of you might say that's what you've been doing this whole time. To a degree you are correct. All of you have been given a lot of slack in letting you take control of your pertinent areas. Take that as a compliment, being trusted like that, because you know Redsaw doesn't trust anybody. Not even me. Now, he has given you permission to work en masse. All territories are not to be taken one from the other. Be content with what you have for what's next is not to be between ourselves, but to finally flood not only the streets, but homes and residences as well. Consider this notice you can go wherever you please and do whatever you please. Any resistance by anybody regardless of who they are or how old are to be eliminated. This is Noah's Flood, ladies and gentlemen. It's time to clear the city of any opposition to Redsaw's rule. Seek them out and remove them however you wish, and be sure to make your message clear."

A smaller, unshaven man in the front with messy brown hair raised his hand.

Charlie looked at him.

"Sir, um . . . after this, what then? Just sit around and enjoy?"

Charlie smirked. "I suppose there's that. By all means, enjoy, my friend, but you're missing the point. The world is watching. If you carry out your tasks properly, you will then make a worldwide statement of what crossing Redsaw will do and, more specifically, what crossing us will do."

"And then?"

"I am only at liberty to share what I'm told to share, and what I stated tonight is what I was told to share. Follow the steps when given steps and once you reach the end of the line, all will become clear." He firmed his tone. "That is all. Go, and do."

Redsaw paced the roof of Owen Tower, every so often looking up at the Doorway above this throne. Truth be told, things were getting a bit boring here in the city. Initial rule and Axiom-man's demise were a triumph and a wonderful high to ride, but, now, things were cooled down.

He just hoped Charlie delivered the message. If he did, then shortly the city would liven up again.

Redsaw took in the Doorway of Darkness. As much as he hated to admit it, all would have to be executed with precision and with the correct timing. If his master found out what he had in mind, he was certain the Doorway would be shut and, worse, he'd lose his power.

He floated up to the Doorway and entered, hovering just inside. Compared to this endless space of swirling red and black clouds, the Doorway was but a pinprick in its overall grandeur.

Redsaw ventured in further. "Master," he said, "all is being conducted as you asked. Thank you for the opportunity to expand my domain."

"*My* domain," his master responded.

"Apologies, my lord. I meant the same."

There was silence.

Now was the time to play timid. "If I may, my lord, how shall your rule come to pass through me in my world?"

The master didn't reply and Redsaw briefly wondered if he had an answer.

Of course he did. He had to.

"I will bestow upon you the ability needed to branch my dominion over the land. You will be its overseer once complete. You must prove yourself. If you do, then more shall be added unto you. If you do not, that which you have will be taken away."

The statement made Redsaw's heart sink. He knew there was no chance for him if he took on the master himself. Obedience was the only option lest he lose his abilities.

Obedience . . . for now.

"Yes, my lord," Redsaw said. He turned to depart but stopped when the master said, "Your servants are almost ready. I can sense the beginnings of the other Door."

"Excellent." Battle Bruiser and Lady Fire, as good as they were, were not always the shiniest tools in the shed. It was pleasant to know they were in the midst of coming through on their task. "What is it that you wish me to do, Master?"

"Return and wait. I will summon you when required and you will know what true power feels like."

Redsaw swallowed his grin. "Yes, Master. As you wish."

Axiom-man stood on the corner of the building and looked down at the six-story drop below. Though Valerie had never fallen, the view of the descent was a mirror of what happened on that rooftop two years ago. It was there she had fallen.

It was there Axiom-man had fallen.

Whatever heights they achieved as a couple plummeted to the ground that day, Valerie having paid the ultimate price.

He sensed Night Fowler approaching. "You don't need to ask if I'm okay. You already know the answer."

"I do."

He turned and stepped toward her. "Aiyesha showed me how to contain what I feel and how to process it, but I must be a poor learner. I can keep the darkness within at bay but it's still there, begging to come out."

"You are being tested in the martial way. Ask yourself: Why do you fight? Not just your battle against the evils of this city, but also the battles within. Have you ever asked yourself that?"

"Only the first part."

"You must understand the second because with that understanding will come wisdom. No one can understand or do it for you, however you were given a guide." She paused. "We know all paths lead to Redsaw. Once we arrive at that point, you cannot beat him until you win the war within yourself."

"Then what's the point of even being here? I don't I think can win. Not after what he's taken, and not just from me, but from so many others."

She stepped up to him so she was only mere inches away. "If you do not win your battle inside, you will not have victory over your enemy. You know how he operates and how he gets his strength. Don't be a source for that. Not you. Especially not you." She sighed and altered her voice to sound more like Katie than Night Fowler. "I know you were not told everything. Please understand your ignorance in some areas are to our advantage. As we head toward our goal, the reasons will unveil themselves and you will appreciate what Aiyesha has done for you by initially withholding."

"Initially?"

"Yes. As of now you were deliberately given only so much information upon which to operate. To have received further, while it might seem like a good idea at first, would have only led to our defeat."

Strategy and critical thinking were drilled into him as Aiyesha ran him through the paces at the Central. He understood what Night Fowler meant: It was about not getting ahead of yourself and putting your mind in the future when it should be in the present. Obviously he was being used, and the feeling sickened him, but not used for terrible reasons just . . . used.

Axiom-man asserted his tone. "When this is done, you can tell her to find another pawn." He walked past her and headed toward the center of the rooftop.

"Is that what you think? That after all this, after these past two years you are viewed as nothing more than a disposable asset? If you do, then you have some serious inside work to do before you're even deemed ready."

"Don't argue with me, Katie."

"Shut up, *Mike*!"

He put his hands on his hips and glanced up. "Is that it? Are you mad because when we first met, I used you to get done what needed doing?"

"No. I know now you were merely conducting your mission and I was a fellow soldier in that regard. Unlike you, I can separate work from my personal life."

"Personal life. Really. What personal life could you possibly have after faking your own death then dedicating the rest of your existence to fighting on the frontlines?"

"You're so naïve. Do you think a personal life is only what people do when they're not working? Grow up. You can still work around the clock and have a personal life. The difference is its internal, not filled with beers and burgers and idiot friends around the table."

"Idiot friends? So, what, you got burned?"

"No. I walked away. I hurt *them* not me. This world needs fixing and since those appointed to help others were being dreadfully slow, I put in to fill in the gap. To speed things up. You did the exact same thing, Gabriel. I'm well aware it was that news article about that little girl that cemented your decision as to what to do with your powers. You were frustrated too and knew you could do something about it. You also knew you couldn't solve everything everywhere all at once, but you did know you could solve things on your own where you could help speed up the process."

How? I never told her a thing about that. Aiyesha! Wait, how would she know unless . . . "He's orchestrating the whole thing, isn't he, my messenger."

She put a hand on his shoulder. "*Our* messenger."

Axiom-man took a moment then nodded. "Okay." He put his hand on her shoulder in return. "Let's finish what we need to do."

Night Fowler nodded.

CHAPTER NINE

IT WAS NIGHT again, rain pouring, but not the rain everyone was used to. This rain came filtered through Redsaw's dark clouds above, carrying with it whatever was in that mix of darkness. When the rain struck the skin, it was like getting pricked with hot water.

Gunn drove through the old neighborhood in the north part of town, windshield wipers whipping back and forth, trying to keep the downpour at bay. He didn't want to be here but he had to.

He pulled up to the curb. Houses out here didn't have driveways and he didn't want to chance it in the back-alley parking behind the house.

Jack drew up his collar, tugged his hat down on his head good and tight, then braced for the rain. "Wait," he said. He patted just under his left armpit for his piece. "'Kay, good." He got out and kept his head down so the rain didn't blow against his face.

The sidewalk leading up to the cement steps to the porch were cracked and uneven. *Wish she had done better. Heh. Look at yourself, Jack.* Now on the porch, he rapped on the screen door twice. He peaked through the small rectangular window beyond the screen door of the door proper.

The lights were out.

He leaned toward the front room window and no light came from over there either. Not that the lights being off were a sign of anything bad. Ever since Redsaw took over the city, standard home practice was stay in and keep things dark lest predators come around.

Jack pounded his fist on the doorframe. "Hey, Kim, it's me. Open up."

No answer.

He banged directly on the screen door. "Yo, Kim. It's Jack. Need to talk."

He checked for his piece again, a moment of security. He also glanced around the front yard and as far up and down the sidewalk as his vision would let him see from where he was. All seemed quiet.

Shoving his hands in his pockets, he shouted, "Hey!"

A moment later, some thumps at the door then the clunky undoing of locks. When Kim opened the door, she looked like hell. Her chin-cropped dirty blonde hair was in static mode, and she had lost a considerable amount of weight since Jack last saw her. When she seemed to recognize him through the screen door, she unlocked it then pulled it open. Jack opened the door the rest of the away.

"You look like an alley cat," he said. It wasn't completely true. Her tight black T-shirt and slightly baggy blue jeans had a hint of charm to them he couldn't quite place.

"Jack?" she said.

"Yeah."

"What's wrong? What's going on?"

"Can I come in?" He looked side to side. "Stayin' out here gives me the creeps."

"Yeah, sure, sure," she said and waved him in.

Once his feet were on the welcome mat inside the door, Kim—Kimberly—made quick work of sealing everything back up.

"Hey," he said.

"Hey." She wrapped her arms around him and hugged him tight. He returned the embrace, something only Kim got. She wasn't his sister, but she sure felt like it. She wasn't a former a lover, but she sure felt like that too. When Jack first started out and hit the beat, Kim was a junkie but not on purpose. She'd been drugged on a bender one night. While passed out, someone shot her up with heroin. When she came around, she was in the midst of its effects. Next thing she knew, she was wandering around looking for a fix anywhere she could get it. Went into some adult work and Jack rescued her from a pimp the department had been following for some time because of the drugs. Kim got clean but never forgot Jack for the rescue. Over the years, though they hardly talked, the bond was always present. Neither one of them could place it especially since they came from opposite worlds, but it was there and it was important, and Kim had secretly helped him put away some people that needed to be in a cell and not on the streets.

Then she passed the baton.

"You okay?" he asked.

"As good as it gets, I suppose."

"Yeah. Look, I shoulda checked up sooner. Lots been going down, as you know, but that ain't no excuse. I'm sorry," he said.

"I should have done the same and . . . and I assumed the same of you. The busy part, I mean."

"Not so much these days, sad to say."

He filled her in on what happened to the force once Redsaw took over. She didn't flinch at anything he said and remained stoic the whole time. He finished with saying, "I need to talk to Josh. He's around, yeah?"

She pressed her lips together then released. "Yeah. Hang on." Kim left the room and headed toward what seemed the direction of the kitchen. Jack didn't know the layout of the house. He seldom came by and when he had, he stuck to the landing and the front room.

Kim came back with a sixteen-year-old beside her, her hand on his shoulder. The kid had dark hair, scrawny, and sported a Metallica T-shirt and baggy jeans. Jack couldn't tell if the kid was starving or just looked that way.

"I need to talk to Josh alone, Kim. He's not in trouble. For safety reasons, the less ears the better." Only now did he realize his sopping hat was still on his head. He took it off and held it as gentlemanly as he could in front of his body.

Kim glanced at Josh then back at Jack, then nodded.

"Thanks," Jack said.

She turned to the kid. "Don't say anything you don't want to, okay?"

Josh nodded.

She kissed the top of his head then left the room.

The old man and young teen stood silent, each with each other's eyes peering into the other's. Jack was curious as to who would break first but it better not be himself. He was a cop, for crying out loud. Stare downs were part of the gig. Some snot-nosed teen wasn't going to beat him at that.

But, dang, was the kid good. It was well over five minutes before Josh briefly glanced away then glanced back. It was then Jack knew he got to him. Good. Authority was needed.

"You're not in trouble, kid. I assured your mom of that. Besides" —he ran a hand over his head— "ain't nobody to get in trouble with these days anyway." He shot out his index finger. "Don't take that as permission to be stupid."

"Tough words for a fat cop," Josh said.

"Yeah? Tough words for a scrawny kid who's lucky I didn't tell their mama what they do when she's not looking."

Josh's voice went gentle. "Thanks for that."

"No problem."

Josh folded his arms and suddenly grew up by a couple of years. "What do you want?"

"I need movement." He knew Josh knew what that word meant.

"There's always movement."

"Yeah, I know, which is why I'm asking you. More specifically, *unusual* movement."

Josh glanced back in the direction his mom went. He held the position like a statue and Jack could only guess he was double checking if his mom was lurking. When he turned back, his voice dropped to a whisper. "I snuck out a couple nights ago. I saw nothing. Just the usual."

"Usual?"

"The same thing you saw on the way over here . . . so nothing."

"Right."

"But I did hear the same two words off and on."

Jack raised an eyebrow.

"The covering."

"Covering." It was more a statement than a question.

"I think a lot of bad people are about to do a lot of bad things."

"Worse than the crap you pull?"

"What I pull is a kid stealing a cookie from the cookie jar. These guys . . . if word is right . . . they're gonna burn the whole kitchen down."

Kim re-entered the room. "You boys done?"

No, Jack thought, but he also knew Kim wouldn't leave Josh again.

When Josh spoke, he was back to being a regular teenager again. "Uncle Jack just had some questions. No issue."

"He better not be in trouble, Jack," Kim said.

Jack plunked his hat back on his head. "Kid like him?" He gave Josh a wink. "Never." He nodded to them both then looked at the door. He thumbed over to it. "Um, Kim, can you unlock the fortress so I can get outta here?"

————

Hands clenched on the steering wheel, Jack headed back to his place. He'd be there in quick order since there was no traffic. Heck, even the traffic lights no longer worked.

"The covering, the covering, the covering," he said. It wasn't completely clear what Josh meant and he wished he could have gotten more information, if there was any, but he got as best he could. His deal with Kim was he could talk to her and to Josh about business but only in very short conversations. She didn't want anything to do with her old life and she knew her kid was a troublemaker so did what she could to keep him out of trouble. Fair enough. Better that than sitting behind some bars. Granted, sometimes Mom Jail was worse than the real thing. At least it had been with Jack's mother.

His windshield shattered in the middle and the whole thing spider-webbed, small pieces of glass bursting out along its frame, contained within the plastic that stopped most windshields from completely shattering.

"Hey!" he shouted as the car swerved. Out of his right eye he caught a sidewalk so pulled over.

The rearview window suddenly shattered as well.

For a second, Jack thought it best to drive away as much as able but he was in no mood. He pulled his gun and opened the driver's door. He firmly planted his foot on the ground and got out, searching around for the jackass that busted up his car.

A loud metallic boom sounded low to the ground on his left. He checked. The back passenger side of the four-door had a wild dent in it. Two feet away? A brick. Jack picked it up and waved it around. "All right, ya louses. Who threw this thing?" He made sure the gun was in plain sight. "Come on! Get out here, losers."

When he turned around to face the car, not far on the opposite side was a crowd of at least ten guys, maybe a couple more.

Jack pointed his gun at them.

A brick that flew in from the side caught him in the cheekbone, sending his head into a dance and he stumbled. A sharp pain blossomed in the back of his knee and the next thing he knew he was close to the ground, kneeled over as if about to pray.

Maybe I should, he thought.

He put both hands on the weapon and looked up as a burgundy brick headed toward his face.

Jack instinctively closed his eyes and braced for impact.

A dull metallic clink sounded.

Jack opened his eyes. The brick was on the ground some ten feet away.

The thugs across from him looked at the brick then looked in the direction of whatever threw it off course.

Two dark gray shadows dropped out of the darkness and landed in the middle of the men. Jack could hardly see through the rain and flurry of motion but two of the guys dropped instantly the moment the shadows appeared. A whirl of gray fabric moved amidst the men in a circle and two more went down.

Jack wished he could see what was going on but the shadows were moving too fast to catch exactly what they were doing. He did notice an arm shoot out from one of the shadows then retract back in a flash while at the same time another thug collapsed at the knees and fell over.

There was some kind of line, bumpy not smooth, that dropped from the hand of one of the shadows. In a spin, that same line was around everyone but the shadows' legs. The next moment, all standing men were on the ground, the line having ripped their feet out from under them. The shadows pounced, hands flew, and it was over.

The two shadows arose amidst the heap of bodies and looked at him.

Jack slowly stepped forward then carefully lowered his gun.

Axiom-man stepped up to him.

"Where'd you learn to do that?" Gunn asked.

"Somewhere else."

Jack arched an eyebrow. Axiom-man's partner came up beside him and Jack took in the figure with a full face mask overshadowed by a hood. The dark gray suit was akin to army fatigues with pouches and a belt. A large dark gray cape draped over the person's frame.

"This is Night Fowler," Axiom-man said firmly.

Great, another whacko, Gunn thought, but then thought better of it. "Um, nice to meet ya. Um, thanks."

Night Fowler nodded.

Jack glanced past the costumed partners to the motionless men on the ground. He didn't see blue light. Didn't see a fantastic display of inhuman strength. Didn't see anybody's feet lift off the ground and stay there. Now he wasn't so sure it was Axiom-man he was dealing with never mind this Night Fowler person. As far as he knew, this whole thing could be a ruse.

But he knew Axiom-man's voice so unless he was dealing with a good imitator, he had no choice but to give a little trust. Cautious trust, but trust nonetheless.

"How'd you know I'd be here or is it just luck?" Jack asked.

"I don't believe in luck," Axiom-man said.

"Are you sure it's you?" Jack asked, the words out of his mouth before he could keep them in.

"Are *you* sure it's me?"

Don't give anything away. No. Just in case. "You'll do for now," Jack said, finally holstering his weapon.

"Get in the car. Go straight to your apartment. Talk to no one. Direct line. Understood?" Axiom-man said.

Jack looked at the men on the ground again. "Yeah. Understood."

CHAPTER TEN

"NOW, EVERYBODY, BE very, very good and listen to the lady," Battle Bruiser said, glock pointed at a crew of men kidnapped from the town. It took a while to locate them but that was only because Lady Fire insisted they ransack the bars first for a drink before rounding up a group of guys who could work a crane. Bruiser wished he had the built-in strength to lift the silver himself but he capped out at about lifting a truck.

Lady Fire approached one of the men and ran a hand under his chin. "You're cute."

Bruiser didn't think so but who was he to criticize the woman's tastes? Yet . . . he didn't like the little swell of jealousy that rose within. Lady Fire was a partner not a lover. Friends for life and all that.

"Now, boys," Lady Fire said, lighting her hands aflame, "all you have to do is work those cranes my friend here was so kind to bring up this rotten hill."

The men stood frozen.

"What? You don't think you owe him since he had brought the bloody things up here in parts."

One guy, about twenty years old, spoke up. He was out of breath.

Wuss, Bruiser thought.

"Ma'am," the guy said, raising a hand as if in class.

"Yes?" she said, raising her flaming hand higher.

The guy looked to the rest of the men. "We're exhausted. We ain't like you. We can't do stuff over and over without . . . without getting tired."

"Hmph." She let loose and sent a fireball straight into the guy. He immediately caught fire and hit the ground, rolling around, trying to douse the flames. When most of the flames were out, Lady Fire blasted him again, this time turning him into a bonfire. His wails echoed throughout the large rocky nooks and crannies of the hill before they went silent.

Two of the other men looked at the fiery corpse; the other two looked away.

"Everyone understand now?" she said.

They all set eyes on her.

Slowly, one by one, they all muttered, "Yes."

"See? Told yas," Bruiser said. "Ya shoulda listened to the lady."

Redsaw debated if he should leave the city alone. If he was going to expand his territory as per his master's blessing, he had no choice but to leave. But if it worked, if all came to pass as the master said, then the temporary leave would be non-issue.

He glanced up at the Doorway. Billows of black smoke poured out, drifting up into the sky as if an offering to his master.

He stepped to the building ledge.

It was time to show the city they might hide indoors but he was still in charge.

Redsaw dove off the building's ledge and headed straight for the ground before a sharp arc upward just before street level. He raced up the side of the heavily-windowed tower opposite his. He sharply bent forward and crashed through the windows about halfway up before yet another dive straight into the office floor.

He plowed through the stories, busting through floor after floor then kicked on the speed and smashed through the ground floor's industrial tiles and floorboards and crashed into Winnipeg Square. He landed hard and firm on his feet. He glanced around; high-hanging signs with arrows showed which direction led to what building up on street level. He saw the white-on-black text indicating the direction of Owen Tower. Not that he needed direction. He knew the underside of all buildings surrounding his own.

Redsaw powered up, his fists bursting into balls of red energy, the intense crimson growing deeper and brighter in color the more energy he poured into them.

This was going to be fun.

Redsaw let his power fill him and enjoyed the pulsating bursts of energy running through his entire body. He closed his eyes and centered himself, clearing his mind until all that was left in his mind's eye was eternal darkness and sheer silence. He breathed in slowly through his nose then out through his mouth.

His eyes snapped open. "Go!"

He took off, fiery lightning exploding out of his fists as he hit the first foundation of the nearest neighboring building to his own. The intense heat of his power melted through the girders as he simultaneously tore through. He banked right and took out another one, then following the rest of the rectangular base in a circle, knocked out the loading-bearing beams that secured the building. Now it was nothing more than a house built on sand.

He turned left, pouring fire out of his fists, crashing through more beams and barriers. Just as he curved in to smash through the drywall concealing another, an elderly homeless lady crossed his path, probably using the Square for warmth.

If you want warm . . . he thought and lit her up as he flew through her body, sending bone and muscle and blood upward in a brilliant display of gooey red mist.

Another girder taken down. Then another and another.

No sound came from the street above, indicating nothing had happened yet. It didn't matter. They were still unstable. All of them.

With an angry screech, Redsaw let loose and criss-crossed this way and that, taking out walls and more supports, flying fast enough to escape the falling debris.

"More, more, more!" he shouted and let the red fires of hell out of his fists.

Windows of the shops in the Square shattered. Dust filled the air in a dense cloud.

Redsaw sharply banked upward, heading straight up through the floors of another building, smashing through level after level until he shot through the top of the building with a violent crash. Now, hovering about thirty feet above that rooftop, out here, it appeared as if nothing happened besides the external damage he caused. He waited. Listened. Paid attention to any inkling the buildings were going down.

They didn't.

With a yell, Redsaw bent forward and shot toward mid-level of the buildings surrounding Owen Tower. Fists firing shots of explosive red energy one after the other, he crashed through the center of the surrounding buildings, blasting apart anything supportive in its middle. When he burst through a shattering of glass on his final round, he headed back up into the air then drifted in the direction of his throne. Behind him, croaks and groans of unsteady metal cracked and droned.

He headed straight for this throne. As he sat, he lifted his arms and pulled on the power of the Doorway, letting its darkness and might fill him through his fingers, hands, arms, and down into his very being.

In a blink, he lowered his hands and clapped them together as hard as he could. Unstoppable red energy poured forth in a violent wave of destruction, taking out the first few floors of the building opposite.

Redsaw drew his hands into himself and let the power reabsorb inward.

Fires and explosions went off in the buildings around.

One boom. Two.

On the third, the building he just hit gave way and the top floors collapsed down on the ones beneath, setting off a chain reaction of utter destruction as the building blew downward toward the ground, dust and debris rocketing upward while the rest of it descended.

Another building creaked and swayed then buckled forward, snapping along its construction and toppling into the building opposite. Immediately upon impact, both buildings began to crumble and then come crashing down, cement and metal and wood and glass all heading to the middle of Portage and Main like an avalanche, piercing the concrete of the intersection and pounding a crater into the asphalt.

All became brown and gray and black dust and smoke, fires and explosions racking the area, Owen Tower standing strong amidst it all.

As tornados of chaos swirled about, hell raging, Redsaw said, "More."

<hr>

The power cut out around 6PM.

A crowd of men and women armed with guns, baseball bats, knives, iron pipes, and other destructive instruments headed down Portage Avenue.

"Is this it?" Axiom-man asked.

"Maybe," Night Fowler replied.

"Looks to be around two thousand people."

"Small portion of the city."

Axiom-man checked again, focusing hard on the furthest edge of the crowd. "I was wrong. More are coming. I don't see an end."

"Then we'll make an end."

The people below began to fan out, groups branching off into the crossing streets, heading into the inner-city neighborhoods.

Axiom-man glanced back to the distant suburbs. If anyone else was out in that direction, he couldn't tell, not in the dark. He turned his attention to the horde below. "How can we stop them?"

"Moths to a flame," she said then jumped off the building ledge.

She always does that. What does she want me to say? Wait for me? He hooked a line to the edge of the building and rappelled down to street level.

Night Fowler crept to the mouth of the alley, remaining in the shadows. Axiom-man was on the opposite side.

The people passing by hooted and hollered, raising their weapons as if raising flags of pride, patriots of destruction.

"Your plan?" Axiom-man asked.

Night Fowler nodded across the street: a busted-open pawn shop with a large window near the door. "Be right back."

He didn't know how she did it, but she smoothly weaved through the horde as if doing a dance between each body, the people too focused on their march to interpret her zipping by them as nothing more than someone crossing their path. She moved so fluidly and quickly that even if you noticed her go by, there wasn't enough time to take in her outfit before she was already hidden behind the next person.

"I need to learn that one," he said.

Night Fowler dove in through the shattered main window of the shop then, a moment later, Axiom-man saw her do a somersault exit out the window and a quick sidestep then a grapnel fire as a line shot up the building next to it and Night Fowler ascended.

She disappeared over the rooftop ledge. Axiom-man decided if she had wanted him to follow suit, she would have invited him along. No. She wanted him here.

The pawn shop exploded in a brilliant bloom of orange and yellow, bricks and debris and dust firing outward into the street and into the horde, sending at least twenty people sprawling onto their stomachs.

All marching slowly stopped, all attention drawn to the explosion.

Moths to a flame, Axiom-man thought. *Let's do this.*

Chapter Eleven

In the mass panic about the pawn shop's blowout, the weaponized marching horde began to scatter, assumingly for safety.

Smoke and flame billowed out of the shop as the place went up in a mountain of fire. Sparks and fiery debris popped and blew out every couple of minutes as the place burned, hitting the buildings beside it.

Axiom-man ran into the horde, hurling a smoke bomb left and another right, deep within to explode on those not fully exposed to the black smoke pouring out of the building.

Axiom-man knew the shadows, knew the dark. Aiyesha forced him to spend the afternoon every day for a week in a black room, the task to move around the striking dummies randomly placed in the room, and work on sensing when one was near before striking it. It took time but eventually he developed acute spatial awareness and sensing when something was near began to become second nature.

Axiom-man grabbed a man from behind, turned his head so his body followed, then hip-tossed him to the street. When the man landed, Axiom-man kept him down by a reserved stomp to the back of his head.

He took another by the arm, folded the person's arm behind them in a joint lock, cranked them in the side of the head then pushed them into the dark. He gave a hard turning kick to a woman's liver then, using the same leg, switched to a high side kick to the head of the man beside her.

Axiom-man ducked, the wind from the oncoming baseball bat kicking on his instincts. He reached, caught the bat by the handle, held it toward the ground, then gave a left hook to the assailant's cheek before bringing the hand back in a backfist and cracking the other side.

Axiom-man took the baseball bat and kept going. He held it close, hands positioned as if holding a bo staff, and used the bat in lieu of one, smashing faces and taking the feet out from under any he caught standing.

This couldn't be all of Night Fowler's plan. He could beat up as many people as he wanted and they'd still keep coming.

She better have something more efficient in mind.

———

A dark hand curled around the corner of an alleyway. Its fingers splayed open and black smoke began to pour out.

———

Axiom-man threw an elbow into one guy's chin just below the lip, sending a shockwave through the guy's nervous system, dropping him. He doubled down with a side kick to another thug who rushed him then blocked a blow from a burly guy who Axiom-man quickly spun, tripped, and sent down hard to the pavement.

Night Fowler was somehow back at street level. When she returned, he didn't know. She was a whirlwind of motion, her gray cloak spinning with her, creating a disorienting tornado of fabric, blocking her assailants' line of sight. Shots were delivered to the guts, kidneys, heads, and necks of anyone she touched. Every blow and strike were executed so quickly and fluidly it appeared she was sometimes in two places at once.

The very sight of the fight got Axiom-man even more energetic and he sent a front kick to the gut of an incoming strung-out woman on who knows what followed by a hook kick across her face, sending her down. He spun and put a palm strike to the cartilage under the nose of another but only hard enough to make the guy's eyes water before a quick pop on the button put him out.

As fun as this was, it couldn't go on forever and no matter how well trained anyone was, there was always a limit as to how many people you could take on all at once.

Axiom-man wasn't sure what his own limit was and now wasn't the time to find out.

He kept his footwork quick and sure, moving as he was taught. Not that he had a choice. Aiyesha had made him spend several days—all day, every day—doing nothing but footwork to cement the muscle memory required, everything from basic sidesteps to quick hops and change overs. To ensure he focused only on his feet, she had tied a thin rope around his forearms and body, locking his arms to his sides so the only moveable limbs were his legs.

He launched a high side kick into the face of another assailant before a sweep behind the knees took the guy's legs out from under him. Axiom-man finished him off with an axe kick to the solar plexus.

Ahead, dark, smoky tendrils snaked their way over the street, wide and dense ropes of shadow circulating the area.

Axiom-man knew that darkness, knew that specific black cloud.

Bleaken.

Those marching began to slow their advance as the black smoke began to overtake them.

Axiom-man searched for Night Fowler. She had just finished throwing someone over her shoulder when she looked his way. He made an obvious glance to the smoke. Her head followed his gaze, paused, turned back and nodded . . . then backfisted someone coming in too close from the rear.

Axiom-man ran toward the smoke, dodging and ducking his way between the horde, ignoring those smashing windows and harassing anyone who wasn't part of this attack. Axiom-man managed to grab one guy away from another but the main focus was on finding Bleaken. And it was getting more difficult as more and more black smoke flooded the streets. Thankfully, the smoke hadn't grown so terrible it covered everything thus eliminating an origin point. Axiom-man kept his eyes on the edges of the streams of smoke while maintaining awareness of his surroundings in his peripherals.

He dug deep and went into a sprint, lungs and breathing just fine thanks to all the endurance drills Aiyesha had put him through. If it had been the him of before running this path, he would have gotten winded several blocks back if he had no aid of his powers to give him a surge of energy.

Axiom-man followed the smoke trail and saw it seemed to come to a stop in a wall of darkness. He looked up and, seven stories above, Bleaken stood with both hands outstretched, waves of darkness coming out of them.

Axiom-man ran into the smoke.

———

Night Fowler tapped the side of her mask, activating the switch that lowered night-vision lenses over her eyes. She had hoped all would go green and she'd be able to make out bodies as clear as day. Instead, the darkness was so thick, the lenses didn't do anything. It was as if the darkness swallowed every possible hint of light available.

She set the lenses back to their original place, grabbed her grapnel out of a pouch on her belt and jogged to the nearest building, slapping her grapnel across a face along the way. At the building's bottom, she launched the line and rode it to the roof. Once she unhooked the line and got everything back into its place on her belt, she gazed over the city streets.

The darkness was rising.

She'd heard of the first time a man named Bleaken blanketed the city in darkness. Now it appeared he was doing it again.

"Chaos. Destruction. Murder. Darkness," she said. "The covering." She scanned the ground for Axiom-man. There was nothing to make out. Besides the shouts and hollers coming from below, she couldn't see him. All she knew was he had headed into the smoke.

She had to trust him. His skills were new. Axiom-man had been taught the same as she albeit she knew more solely due to more time spent with Aiyesha. It would be nice if their teacher was here but she knew Aiyesha couldn't interfere. It was on them.

Wherever this smoke was coming from, Night Fowler hoped Axiom-man was at, or near, the source.

She glanced to the street below and despite the darkness filling the streets, she spotted a man bending a woman over the trunk of a car.

Infuriated, she leapt off the ledge.

Chapter Twelve

Bleaken was silent. No words. No laughing. No auditory expression of any kind. Black smoke poured out of his hands and filtered lower and lower to the city streets below.

At the far corner of the roof, far behind him, Axiom-man kept low, slowly drawing his steps in a slight circle to the side. Each foot planted was careful not to disturb the dust and debris most rooftops accumulate. There had to be no sound. Not even a breath.

Once he was aligned with Bleaken, he stood, drew his hands up into a firm, yet calm, guard and carefully traversed the distance, each footfall silent. Besides, Bleaken seemed too interested in what he was doing. What was always puzzling about Bleaken was it seemed his access to spreading darkness was limitless. It was as if his whole body was a constant generator of dense, dark smoke. Axiom-man supposed Bleaken's powers were akin to his own in that way.

Slowly, Bleaken drew one hand down so it was waist level and rotated his wrist so his palm faced Axiom-man. Swirls of black smoke headed Axiom-man's way yet Bleaken never turned his head or the direction of his gaze.

He's knows I'm here, Axiom-man thought, *or, at least, that someone is.* He was close, too, a mere eight or so feet. The smoke pouring out of Bleaken's hand and blanketing the rooftop in darkness picked up pace and billows and billows of smoke blanketed the roof in darkness.

Axiom-man kept moving forward, ears perked for any indication of movement on Bleaken's part. If the man was still coating the rooftop in smoke, it was difficult to tell.

Axiom-man stopped. If nothing changed, he was about three feet away. He listened.

Carefully.

Silence.

He moved in, meaning to put Bleaken in a rear-naked choke and knock him out, but the movement clasped nothing but black air. Something came in from . . .

Axiom-man's right arm snapped up in a forearm block, clashing with what would have been a fist to his face. He quickly grabbed the arm and ran his hand up it until his grip was near the wrist. With a violent jerk, he tugged the arm down. From the shape, he deduced he had Bleaken's right hand, which meant that side was open.

Axiom-man came in with a hook, missed, but doubled back with a backhand and connected hard with the side of Bleaken's head. Locking his grip, Axiom-man didn't let go despite the man still pouring more and more black smoke out of his hands. He had Bleaken with his own right hand so reached in with his left, hooked under the elbow, slipped behind him, and forced Bleaken to bend forward at the waist right as Axiom-man cut to the left and delivered a hard shot to what he hoped was Bleaken's kidney. Based on impact, he struck the floating ribs instead.

Good enough, he thought and plowed blow after blow into Bleaken, railing away as fast and hard as possible. A loud series of snaps informed him the job was complete, which meant, if Bleaken hadn't mutated into something other than a human with abilities, the man should be in severe pain and having difficulty breathing.

A hard boot struck Axiom-man's knee, forcing it to bend inward. Fortunately, he was able to pull it back before full impact but the impact was enough to create a small sprain. He took the shot, ignored it, slowly bent the struck knee just enough so it would stay locked but not enough so he might further the injury, then swept in with his right foot behind Bleaken's and with a violent ridge-hand to Bleaken's neck, followed the strike through so Bleaken stumbled backwards and hit the rooftop.

A violent wind of black smoke burst through the darkness and threw Axiom-man back . . .

. . . and over the edge.

———

The man's face vanished into darkness the moment Night Fowler struck him across the jaw. She followed up with another hook from the other hand, clipping him somewhere in the dark. She swung again, missed, a second later the sound of his body hitting the cement.

She looked around and there was nothing but black smoke in all directions.

What is happening up there? she thought. She went for the night vision lenses in her mask again and clicked them on. They slid into place, but revealed nothing. *Broken.* She fiddled with the switch, her sensitive ears picking up the subtle hum of the thin and narrow mini power pack hidden alongside the switch. They were on yet all she saw was sheer black.

Then she remembered.

Bleaken.

She had only been training on her own at the time, not yet part of the crusade, when he first struck. It took some time, but Axiom-man defeated him and got him out of the public's way by, as the papers called it, "Private imprisonment."

Somebody got out, she thought. She quickly swept her right foot forward and spun to the side when she sensed someone coming near. Rapid footfalls indicated this person was running. Why they were running in the dark, she didn't know, most likely panic. If anything, the darkness was so thick any reasonable person would stay where they were and not move, but the footfalls on the sidewalks and the occasional metallic crunch of cars bumping hard into each other said otherwise.

Night Fowler glanced up, hoping maybe the dark was thinner up there.

It wasn't.

Guard up, she slowly made her way to her left as that's where the nearest building was. She reached out and a few moments later, her gloved fingertips found the wall.

Straight up. She produced her grapnel, ran her hand up the wall, then fired after attaching the gauntlet on her wrist. Listening carefully, the whir of the cord firing out and ascending became her only focus. There was a quiet *clink* far away and high up. *Confirm the—*She stopped the thought. Next step was confirm the hold on the object of ascension but she couldn't see a thing. The best she could do was tug on the cord. Seemed secured, but she couldn't risk it. She drew it out enough so she could turn around, run the cord over her shoulder, and then try to make off with it from the building. Night Fowler got what felt like six inches of movement before the line wouldn't budge.

She stepped up the wall and activated the gauntlet, letting the cord draw her up to wherever its hooked end latched on. She went slowly so as to not stress the line in case it didn't find full solid purchase but it seemed to be solid enough to bring her up. The line stopped. With her other hand she felt around for the grappling hook. It had lodged itself between a clunky series of bricks at an awkward angle between the lip of the ledge and the building proper. No matter. She put both hands onto the ledge than pulled herself up and over, careful to remain just beside the edge once on the roof.

Using nothing but her sense of touch and visualization, she found the hook, pried it loose, then reassembled it back into the gauntlet as she stood.

There was nothing but darkness all around. It was no better than the street.

And Axiom-man was somewhere in this.

She didn't know where and the unmistakable sound of an explosion went off somewhere below.

———

The rush and speed of the wind blowing past Axiom-man's head and body as he fell was enough to trigger panic. He thought of *shifting* and turning on his powers . . . but if he did that, he might become a beacon and Redsaw would come and there'd be a fight. He reached into the long pocket on the inside of his forearm.

A grappling hook. Small, folded. The moment he pulled it out, it snapped to life and three prongs sprang forth from the center. He yanked on the rope coiled up inside the pocket, loosening it, and hurled the grappling hook.

This is not going to . . . . A metallic *clink* rang out, the line went taut, and Axiom-man stopped falling with the jolt.

Immediately after its catch, the line let loose and he fell again, his hands still on the rope, his body now somewhat vertical, and the dreaded knowledge that, at any moment in this place of black smoke, he'd break his legs on impact—or worse.

Harsh scraping drew his attention slightly upward and the line went tight again. His body jerked the second things rammed to a stop and he swung left and right until, just before knowing he'd have to *shift* to save his life, he fell again. The thought of *shifting* despite the extreme risk vanished and the all-consuming thought of falling to his death despite knowing he could fly filled his mind. Heart racing, a cacophony of clinks and clanks above and then silence.

The line went tight; one hand was jerked free, his remaining hold on the line nothing more than his index and middle fingers and thumb.

The line collapsed and the wind rushed and he knew any second he'd—he went limp and hit the pavement face down, his fisted forearms beneath to help absorb the shock of the fall and shield his head. The microsecond after impact, he splayed out, sending as much impact energy outward as possible.

He couldn't move.

Chapter Thirteen

REDSAW BLASTED INTO the black smoke knowing full well Bleaken was in charge of this area, and right now, flying blind was a good thing. Redsaw lit up his fists, the fiery red energy illuminating the area around him, giving him a hazy view of the streets beneath.

Let them burn, he thought and let loose with all he had, each blast of red power striking every vehicle he caught sight of.

Explosions lit up the dark, the roar and rush of flames firing through car after car as he poured it on, each car triggering another to explode in a vast array of metal and plastic and shards of glass.

Petro Canada. Gas station.

Redsaw flew over and brought his hands together as if praying but pointed his fingers downward, concentrating a beam of violent red energy, busting through the ground and straight into the gasoline depositories beneath.

The entire street shook then broke open when a violent eruption of fire scorched outward like a volcano.

Buildings rocked in their places. Winnipeg was not built for earthquakes. Not out here on the Prairies.

Redsaw aimed his arms outward to either side and sent blasts of power through the buildings as he flew past, cutting them wherever the beams landed, some merely getting a shave off the top while others were pierced straight through the middle.

Another gas station. Another fireball.

The whole place went sky high as flames roared through the area, the ground breaking and shaking from the violent explosion. Buildings cracked and tumbled downward, the horrific screams of those burning alive filling the air and imbuing Redsaw with more and more power. Each soul leaving Earth was one more life to add to his body count and build himself bigger and stronger and more powerful than ever before.

He was well past Bleaken's smoke by now but that didn't erase the thick gray and black smoke and thousands of pounds of dust and dirt filling the area. Even if someone wasn't killed by the fire or the quake, smoke inhalation alone would do them in.

Redsaw spun around in the air and headed back toward the city proper.

There was more to do.

All Axiom-man could think about was the coffin he awoke in after being transported to the Central after first trying to take down Redsaw.

Now, it was dark all around and his arms and hands were beneath his chest. He wanted to move but his brain didn't seem able to send the signal to his limbs to get them going. Did he break them? No. He'd be in agonizing pain if all four limbs were broken in just one spot, never mind several.

I'm paralyzed! he thought, his heart jumping into a panic. He blinked his eyes open and closed.

Bleaken was still in charge of the dark.

"I could float," he whispered, but that would demand turning his powers on and, again, would end up summoning Redsaw, and he was in no condition to face him right now.

He peered left and right, as if moving his eyeballs was some sort of affirmation all would be okay.

Concentrating, he slowly moved his head side to side then froze when he heard voices. He listened for footsteps in case someone was coming near, but they sounded a far enough distance off that whoever it was probably didn't even know he was there.

He closed his eyes.

The coffin.

This was no different.

Axiom-man sunk inward, pulling his energy together and gathering it deep within his system and channeling it muscle by muscle to his forearms.

He took three deep breaths through his nose as his countdown then breathed out as hard as possible as he forced himself to command his elbows to bend and move. With a big push, he lifted himself half a foot up. He breathed in again and exhaled hard until he was able to roll his fists onto the pavement and brace himself.

Catching his breath, he did a quick body scan, attempting to sense if everything worked.

He straightened further and was on his knees. Bones throbbing, muscles stinging with bruises, he slowly exhaled when he acknowledged he was in one piece, not dead. Somehow, he had gotten himself to the ground without breaking a bone. Mild or even severe cuts could be dealt with but he needed his skeleton to work so he could continue.

It took almost five full minutes but he got to his feet and stumbled to the side, falling into a building wall that suddenly popped up out of the dark.

Don't go down, he thought. A whisper: "Don't go down."

He leaned against the wall, adjusting and shuffling his footing so he was more stable. He wasn't sure how much time had passed until he was relatively sturdy and the spinning in his head stopped to a level that enabled him to function.

Night Fowler. I need my partner. Partner? No. Not Katie. She was too young. *No, not like that,* he told himself. *A friend. Ally.* "Help."

The walkie-talkie on his belt crackled. "Axiom-man."

Katie! "Yeah."

"Where are you?"

He tried to think, tried to remember the area before all went dark and before his fall. "I don't know. I'm sorry."

"You weren't paying attention."

"I almost died."

"Oh."

"Yeah."

"Stay where you are. I'm coming. I'll use your tracker and—"

"No. I'll come to you. If you're in the smoke, find a way out. I'll do the same and then we'll coordinate a rendezvous point."

"Copy."

The line went silent.

Now which way was out?

This all was familiar. Some said déjà vu wasn't real. Well, if that was true, Redsaw wouldn't be heading directly for the suburbs. Last time he made the effort to use suburbia as a source of power, he had held back . . . to a point. At the time, setting a basic fire was the best he could manage. Now, with his powers amplified thanks to continually being around the Doorway of Darkness, he had a better idea. And it wouldn't take much.

Fortunately, greenery was mandatory on suburban streets. So were parks.

And parks had forests.

He was north of downtown, heading over a middle-class area with neighborhood parks and tree-lined streets. Even backyards had trees and shrubbery and, for some, very dry grass. Redsaw didn't hesitate when he was over the first park he saw. He flew over where the forestry was the densest and let loose ball after ball of fiery red power, igniting the trees. He circled around the park just above the tree line, ensuring each dump of raw red energy struck its mark. The branches went up instantly like dry kindling, the trunks taking a moment to feed off the heat to finally catch aflame. All Redsaw needed to do was make sure he poured it on with as much intense heat as possible.

The trees went up like candles, transforming themselves from shelters for birds and small prey to wild torches, the forest a massive birthday cake.

He flew over the yards and dumped fireball after fireball into as many as possible, even hurling some up over the rooftops until it landed in a yard far off like the perfect basketball swoosh.

Alarms sounded as the smoke and fire piled up, the inferno sweeping the area, the wooden fences alit with flame, imprisoning any inside the houses and leaving them no method of escape.

Redsaw listened for sirens—but heard none. All were busy with the chaos downtown. Those who still stood against him, that was.

Another forest-filled park below. He flew over it, red-hot power spilling from his hands as he rotated through the air like an arrow spiraling toward its target. Every piece of wood his power touched went up instantly.

Redsaw rose higher into the sky to take a look at his handiwork, the screams and shouts and wails of grief below getting quieter and quieter the higher he ascended. Billows of black and gray clouds of smoke burst and rose from the inferno.

It wouldn't be long until the power of the flames would create its own weather and destroy them all.

———

Axiom-man turned a corner and blocked a gray fist that shot out of the shadows.

Night Fowler.

"Easy, it's me," Axiom-man said.

"Sorry. Instinct. Heightened. Especially with what's going on."

He nodded. They were a half kilometer away from the perimeter of Bleaken's covering of darkness.

"Somehow they're navigating in there," she said, "those causing trouble."

Gun shots rattled off not far from where they were. Axiom-man stepped forward as if to go toward it but Night Fowler stopped him. "We're better off out here."

"I don't care about us."

"I wasn't talking about us," she said then looked farther down the street as what civilians were left scrambled farther and farther away from the carnage.

Axiom-man looked at the black smoke and gestured toward it. "So, what, leave them there to die?"

"They're already dead," she said with sorrow.

His heart sank. Despite all the effort, despite getting in there to help, Redsaw had won. He was the one who let Bleaken out and now lives were lost.

"I've seen this before," he said.

"Yeah, last time Bleaken attacked the city."

"Not what I mean. A sudden barrage of death." He looked her square in the eye. "A body count."

"You mean—"

"What were you told about Redsaw?"

She took a moment before replying. "I asked Aiyesha repeatedly about him. She wouldn't talk about it . . . but not in the way you'd think. It wasn't about a bad experience. The look on her face said otherwise. It said, *You don't want to know.*"

"And?"

"I tried pressing her but once her mind is made up, there's no reversing course. But I did bring it up one more time after, when you were in the coffin."

The coffin again. "And?"

"She said we had to make sure you got out of that box otherwise Earth would become his."

He thought for a moment and replayed the words in his mind. "Anything else."

"No."

"You sure?"

"Certain."

He stepped up to her. "I need to find him."

"Is now the time?"

"The city is in darkness and there's a glow way over down that way. It's orange, which means fire. He and I have done this before."

"And?"

"He opened the Doorway of Darkness."

"And changed everything."

Axiom-man nodded.

"Then we need to be careful."

"Very."

Chapter Fourteen

"ALL RIGHT, LET'S keep this simple," Lady Fire said. "The tubs are already the molds. I'm gonna fire up and melt everything to make the forms. It'll take time to cool enough for handling. According to the boss, the strength of the beams isn't an important factor. He said they'd be strengthened a different way, whatever that means."

"Right, gotchya," Bruiser said.

"Stand back."

He took one giant step away.

Lady Fire eyed the tubs. "Let there be fire!"

***

It took some time, but the silver beams had been lifted and set into position the same way they were around Redsaw's throne in Winnipeg. The men who worked the cranes and straps and chains were off to the side, most on the ground on their backs, exhausted.

Bruiser was pretty sure he heard one guy snoring. "Wuss," he said.

He stepped up to Lady Fire underneath the main assembly of the beams. He put his hands on his hips and took a glance around at them. After a soft whistle he said, "Not bad." To Lady Fire: "Hope it's on par with the specs."

"Of course it's on par," she said. "Instructions were to follow the plans to the finest detail."

"And that's been done?"

"Complete."

Battle Bruiser smirked. "Well done, my lady."

She swatted him in the chest. "I'm *not* your lady."

"Girlfriend?"

"What's wrong with you?"

Sheepishly, Bruiser took off his hat. "You."

———

Axiom-man and Night Fowler stayed at the far end of the roof of the Bank of Montreal building. Up here, it was far enough away from Bleaken's ever-expanding blanket of black smoke on the city and far enough away from the top of Owen Tower where Redsaw made his abode.

"Doesn't it strike you as odd that Redsaw chose Oscar Owen's building as his seat of power?" Night Fowler said.

"Highest point in the city," Axiom-man said. "Only Redsaw would want to be seated above everybody else."

"And Oscar?"

"Probably dead or under some sort of coercion to supply Redsaw with all he needs."

"According to the newsfeed that ran at the Central while you were training, Oscar Owen was active for a time in calling out law enforcement for mobilization against Redsaw. Then he just vanished, as if gone into hiding."

"Then more evidence for dead," Axiom-man said. "Or, maybe, rich enough to have a grand plan of escape to get out of the city undetected should something like this happen."

"Doesn't sit right," Night Fowler said.

"It never sits right with the rich."

"Not that. Just . . . something feels off. Can't quite place it and don't have time to think about it." She glanced over at Owen Tower then pointed. "That is our priority. We need to shut that portal down." She turned to him. "Ideas?"

"Last time I used my own power to seal the door, closing it up like doing up a zipper."

"I know," she said.

"What?"

"I know."

"How—"

"While you trained with Aiyesha, I was studying. Access to all you've done is available at the Central."

He didn't like the idea of her reading up on him, but at the same time understood this was the game now and he had an ally, and it made sense she would explore things in full. Katie was always about the fight, whether physically or mentally or any other way a person could undergo a battle. He could only imagine the ferocity of her internal battles, the kind that would set a very young lady on a path toward seeking justice at every turn. She wasn't like him. She wasn't visited by the messenger or given strange powers. She was just a girl with a past that took it upon herself to make things right that had gone wrong. An entire life dedicated to one thing: Justice.

"I don't think we can rely on the past for this one," he said.

"Agreed," she said. "It'll serve as a guide. This is different now. *You're* different. *He's* different."

"He seems unstoppable," Axiom-man said.

"For now."

A red streak flew overhead, its brightness sharply contrasting against the dark sky.

"He's back," Axiom-man said quietly.

"Then, for now, we monitor, notate, and wait until he's in range and away from that portal."

"So be it."

———

Redsaw flew up to his throne, facing it; his knees brushed against the top of the ornate structure. Wells of power surged through him as the deaths of all those he just executed caused his body to throb and vibrate as if about to burst.

He floated closer to the Doorway of Darkness . . . then went in.

"It is done," he said as he hovered there in the murk of endless red and black clouds.

When the master spoke, his voice was firm—even terse—but carried with it a touch of calm. "Receive."

The outer rims of the doorway proper began to curve inward, heading into the realm of black and red. The corners elongated and came at Redsaw like tendrils of an octopus reaching for its prey in the dark depths of the ocean. Each corner latched onto Redsaw's wrists and ankles, stretching his body out like a X. A rush of wind roared behind him. He glanced over his shoulder to see a tightly-wound black cloud swirling with red spiraling out of the void toward him. One moment, it was way out off in the beyond, the next, nearly upon him.

Then the black cloud encased his entire body, endless night swirling around him, over him, and under him, the cloud shedding its own vibrations of power and authority.

At first, it was just his muscles and bones drawing in and filling up with that black and red power, but soon . . . soon it reached deeper. Far deeper. Inside. The heart. The spirit. His core being. It was as if the cloud was trying to pry its way into his inner self, the essence of who he was.

Time slowed. Maybe not in reality but at least for him.

"I am the master," the voice said.

Redsaw's mind flashed to his own desire to be just that one day, but it seemed with the master inside him or a portion thereof, thinking so would not be wise so he shoved the thought out of his head.

"You are the master," Redsaw said. The surge of energy pounded at the door to his soul, beat after beat, knock after knock, intensifying with each rap.

Dark.

Black.

And Redsaw knew he had to let his master in.

"*You* are the master," Redsaw said quietly, stunning even himself because he wasn't sure that involuntary utterance came from him or if his master forced it. It didn't matter.

The master entered and a violent surge of power and might filled Redsaw, coursing through him, forcing him to shake and violently jerk about. The tendrils kept him in place as the darkness all around began to fade just enough for him to see he was still in the void but glowing and humming with red energy.

The black tendrils gripped his wrists and ankles so tightly he thought his hands and feet would go numb from lack of circulation. Instead, he felt his hands being drawn together and his body tilting forward.

There, over there, was the Doorway's opening.

"Go," the master said.

"Go," Redsaw whispered.

He flew, wrists and ankles still entwined with the black cloud. He burst out into the night air and soared into the sky, crackles of violent red energy roaring up and down within him.

As he flew north, he drew the inner power of the Doorway out and brought it along the sky, a terrifying horizontal tornado of swirling red and black darkness, a spiraling funnel of power.

The beginning.

Axiom-man and Night Fowler looked up as the Doorway of Darkness blew out atop Owen Tower, a streak of red energy ripping across the sky and pulling with it a whirlwind of black and red clouds.

Thunder rumbled and boomed simultaneously.

Screams and shouts added to the cacophony of chaos.

"What's . . . happening?" Night Fowler asked.

Axiom-man analyzed the dark, smoky line of power racing across the sky and out of the city. "I don't know."

CHAPTER FIFTEEN

REDSAW HAD NEVER flown faster in his entire life. He had hit high speeds before, almost three hundred kilometers an hour, but nothing like this. There was no way to measure but if he had to ballpark it, doing four hundred or five hundred kilometers an hour wouldn't be a stretch. No matter. All it meant was he would reach his destination sooner than anticipated.

He lit up the sky in a brilliant beam of red light, pulling behind him the four corners of the Doorway of Darkness with each of his limbs. Far below, a hazy shadow overcame every area he passed over, yet up here, the width of the power he dragged was as wide as his arms could outstretch.

He could only suspect things were going to get a lot bigger once he touched down. He just hoped Battle Bruiser and Lady Fire did their part.

———

Lady Fire lay on her wings, using them as a makeshift cushion against the rocky ground.

"I'm bored," she said.

Battle Bruiser stood there, facing her, his gaze fixed on—she didn't know.

"Would you stop doing that?" she said.

He remained still.

"Bruiser!"

He snapped to attention and set his eyes on hers. "What?"

"Cut it out."

"Cut what out?"

She sighed and laid her head back down. "Men."

"Hey," he said, pointing a finger her way, "don't do that."

"It's not like it's not true. You just proved it."

"Yeah, but—"

"No 'yeah, buts.'"

"But?"

She cut him short with a curt, "Shht."

He merely shook his head and faced the opposite direction. And stared at nothing.

The minutes ticked by, each one seeming to take twice as long. Lady Fire figured she'd be more entertained watching water boil than waiting for—

A low rumble echoed above and somewhere far off.

"Great. Now it's going to rain," she said. She looked to Battle Bruiser. He hadn't moved. She put a hand over her eyes. "And I don't think the genius there is going to be of any help."

After a moment of silence, Bruiser said, "It's only water."

"Thanks for joining the conversation." She expected him to face her, but he never did.

More rumbling above and the low, low drone of thunder as if about to explode but never did.

She sat up, straightened her suit a little, then stood and finished fixing herself so she was presentable in costume again. She loved her skin-tight outfit. Just a pain when it came to eating habits and exercise. *Stupid societal pressures on women.* She walked in front of Battle Bruiser and put her hands on her hips. "Do you think I'm fat?"

His eyes widened. "Um, is this a trick question?"

She slapped his shoulder as the rumble intensified. "No, I'm serious."

"It's a dumb question."

"But I'm asking it."

"It's dumb because you shouldn't care how that outfit makes you look," he said. "If you like wearing it, then wear it. That simple. Your beauty is elsewhere. No, wait, that came out wrong. What I meant was—"

"No, we're good. Leave it." She turned away then said, "And you're right."

Thunder cracked overhead and a bright red beam appeared in the sky, heading straight for them.

"That him?" Bruiser said.

"No, it's Santa Claus."

He put his hand just above his eyebrows as if to see better. "That ain't Santa."

"No, but it looks like he's bringing a gift."

Redsaw's world was nothing more than a realm of black and red light, the world beyond hardly visible behind all the power surging around him.

There. The five beams. Hit center.

With a shout, he ripped in amid the columns and landed between them. A bubble of red energy burst out around him. He leaped straight up and brought the streams of black cloud around his wrists to the top center where the beams met. The clouds snapped off his wrists and latched onto the center of the beams like a magnet. The next two from his ankles tore away and streaked down to the bases of two of the other beams. Caught in the center, Redsaw coursed with red power, his body pounding and throbbing as the violent energy circulated through him.

All red power pulled away from the clouds and the beams drove deep into him, filling him to the brim.

Then all went completely black and . . . silent.

Ears ringing from the sudden absence of sound, Redsaw grunted and collapsed back to the ground, landing on his hands and knees like a beast just let out of its cage, ready to kill.

With a violent shriek, he outstretched his arms and howled.

Ream after ream of electric red power spiraled outward and latched onto the beams like a spider trying to climb upward, crackling and launching deafening thunder into the air.

———

All was quiet. Dark. No sight. No sound.

Axiom-man tapped his foot on the ground and didn't produce a noise. The screams of the people stopped. Bleaken's outpour seemed to cease too.

"Night Fowler," he said but was met with no reply. He felt around in the dark, found a shoulder, tested it to see if it was Night Fowler's outfit. It was.

A hand went on top of his . . . and squeezed tight.

———

The silver beams quickly heated up and glowed red, endless power raging out of Redsaw and fueling their charge.

Redsaw grunted. Sweated. Allowed his body to be racked with convulsion after convulsion as the power left his body and fired up the beams. As more poured out of him, the dark began to lift . . . and finally sound returned.

Beyond the pillars he caught sight of Battle Bruiser and Lady Fire laying unconscious on the ground; their bodies must have been thrown far from the initial blast.

But their deaths could power this more, he thought. He wanted to kill them, to expand the energy outward and destroy their pathetic bodies . . . but he couldn't. Could not interfere with the master's plans.

The large black streak of cloud he dragged over to the pillars thundered and roared, red lightning crackling and flashing amidst it.

It burst outward east and west and went on for miles in both directions.

With a final burst of power, his body went rigid as all was dumped from him and into the beams.

Red lightning lit up the land and made it all look as if an inferno.

And in the sky, encompassing as far as the eye could see, a Doorway of Darkness opened across the land.

Chapter Sixteen

Axiom-man's heart dropped and his insides went hollow when the sky above transformed into a chaotic mosaic of red and black clouds. Though he couldn't be sure, he thought he saw red lightning far off into the east.

"What just happened?" Night Fowler asked.

Heart rate rising, Axiom-man reverted inward and practiced his breathing, slowing things down and activating his sympathetic nervous system to calm the panic. When he tried to speak, his voice caught in his throat. "He . . . he opened it. I mean open-opened it. The Doorway. The . . . the . . . . I don't know what this is."

"It's over everything," she said. "The world?"

"I don't know. I hope not. Even this" —he glanced up and pointed— "this is too big. There's no way to close it." *Is there?* "This is not at all what I closed when I first started. This is different."

"Different . . . but same thing?"

He looked her way. She was always difficult to read and her having a mask on right now didn't make it any better. "I honestly don't know."

They gazed out onto the city. Not only did the Doorway of Darkness cover over everything in sight, but plumes of black smoke rose in various parts of the city. Entire buildings had come down. Rubble and dust and bodies littered the streets.

There was no sign of Bleaken either.

He got away, Axiom-man thought. He grit his teeth together. If he had only used his powers, he could have stopped Bleaken, could have stopped the darkness and chaos. But there was a price: Redsaw would come. *But if I* had *activated and if he* had *come, then maybe the Doorway wouldn't be over us right now.* "I missed my chance," he said.

"What chance?"

"To stop him."

Night Fowler remained silent and her quiet was answer enough. Then she said, "You don't know that."

"Deductive reasoning, Katie!" he shouted. She didn't flinch when he said her real name. He calmed himself with a deep breath. "What if I had called him over before this? What if we fought and I won? None of this" —he waved his hand around— "would have occurred. None!"

"You don't know that."

"Stop saying that."

"But you don't."

"So help me I'll—"

"You'll what? Hit me. Try. Your arm would be broken before you even twitched."

She had him there. Despite his grueling time with Aiyesha, Katie had been with her longer and he knew what she could do if pressed.

"I'm sorry," he said. "Now . . . frankly, now we're fu—"

"Think!" she said. "What can we do right now to fix this or at least try to?" She crossed her arms and went silent. He knew she'd stay frozen like that until he came up with an answer.

I'm not ready for this, he thought. "I—"

Night Fowler didn't move, didn't speak.

"I don't even know if stopping him would stop *this.*"

She offered nothing. Was she under instruction to leave this all to him? How far did her servitude to Aiyesha reach? What bargain did she make for the training? *No, can't think like that. You're upset. You feel defeated. You can't walk away. You don't want to walk away. This is it. Now. Today.*

This moment. "I have no choice," he whispered. He looked her in the eye.

Her eyes met his.

"I have to call him."

———

Redsaw slowly floated to the ground in the middle of the beams, the second Doorway of Darkness crackling with red energy and howling with the wind inside it open above him. When his feet touched down, he immediately wanted to get into the air and fly again, his body pulsing with a severe urge to use his power.

Somewhere a ways off on the other side of the triangular structure, he made out two bodies slowly approaching, one large, one small. He knew who they were but didn't bother remembering their names. Just pawns. Nothing more. When he was sure all was in hand, he'd eliminate them. Until then, they would serve.

High above, the Doorway ran along the sky, casting the ground in a dark crimson light, the colors distorted forever.

As they should be.

The task was complete. The Doorway was opened over what he imagined was at least the entire province.

There was no doubt the phenomenon was being broadcasted by someone from somewhere, the whole world tuned into the transformation of a landscape into something much more suitable for his master and . . . himself.

Above, thunder rumbled, banged, rumbled again. Fingers of red lightning spiked out of the Doorway, tickled the ground, traveled along it, retreated back into the Doorway then back out again.

"You can come through," Redsaw said, intending for his master to hear.

He watched the sky, thought maybe some ethereal figure would reveal itself and descend like a mighty god from the heavens to have its way on earth.

There was no response.

The red hue cast upon the fields, hills, and rocks grew darker, so dark it was almost black—then flashed bright, then went dark again.

A violent red tornado dropped from the Doorway and hit the ground, its path seemingly prechosen as it began ripping through anything in its way. Trees split, the surface of the lake far to the left sprung to life in mighty waves from the ferocious wind of the very thing.

Then just as suddenly as the tornado appeared and touched down, it was sucked back up into the Doorway above.

"Intruder," his master said, the voice echoing across the sky. It wasn't a shout. Wasn't a cry. It was a statement.

Intruder? Redsaw thought. No man or woman could go near the Doorway whether here or atop Owen Tower without succumbing to fear. There was no way anyone could have—

Redsaw tore into the sky and, filled with rage and power, flew as fast as he could back to his throne in the city.

Night Fowler surveyed the aftermath below.

Winnipeg was gone.

The entire place was nothing but heaps of rubble, fallen buildings, bodies, fires, debris—death.

The Doorway roared above, it's presence alone unsettling the soul and inducing ever-increasing panic.

Night Fowler retreated inward to calm herself. Breathing in slowly through her nose and out her mouth, she moved from one side of the rooftop to the other, all four sides used to see the damage below.

There was no coming back from this. Not in the same way.

And it would take a long time.

That was . . . if Redsaw was stopped.

———

It didn't take long for Redsaw to be back in the city, the sudden surge in power enhancing his speed.

He landed in front of his throne, took a look at the silver chair, then beyond to the Doorway of Darkness above. It didn't appear different.

He carefully eyed the roof, glancing around, the brightness from the Doorway casting a red hue on the entire rooftop, not a shadow anywhere.

There was no one here.

A sharp, clean, low whistle on the wind from behind.

He spun around, fists raised. A set of bolas wrapped themselves around his ankles.

"Of course you understand," he said to the unknown intruder, "you are dead."

He zapped the bolas off his ankles and walked down the steps to the roof proper.

Another glance around only to reveal no one. If there was anyone up here without invitation—and there clearly was—he'd kill them for the trespass.

A sharp prick hit the side of his neck like a vicious mosquito bite. He brought his hand to it and felt a short, sharp protrusion sticking out of his neck. He pinched it and pulled it out. Nothing but a black needle no bigger or thinner than an eyelash.

The world began to spin.

Chapter Seventeen

Redsaw howled as he fell to his knees. He set his arms outstretched and poured out a flurry of red energy from his hands, swiping their beams this way and that, hoping to hit anyone that was up here without welcome.

His head swooned. Whatever he had been hit with acted fast. A poison? Probably. Some sort of drug, at any rate. It didn't matter. The issue was if or when it would wear off. He hoped his powers or even his innate human charge of adrenaline would blast his metabolism through the roof and he could process it in short order.

If it wasn't fatal, that was.

He set his hands down so he was on all fours, trying to stay alert. "I've . . ." The word hardly came out. He took a deep breath. "I've . . . won. You . . . you're . . ."

A black-slippered foot with a small split in the toes filled his vision before the foot rose up and knocked him in the forehead. Redsaw's head snapped back. He brought it back down again, searching for the foot.

It was gone.

With a grunt, he pushed up off the rooftop and floated so he was upright. He shook his head, the cobwebs slightly loosening. He scoured the rooftop for his assailant. There was nowhere to hide. The entire roof was bathed in red light.

A sharp pain struck his ear even through his cowl and something hard fell to the ground. Hand on his ear, he glanced down. Looked no bigger than a marble.

"Primitive," he said. Another sting rocked his other ear. He let out a shout and lit up his fists. "Show yourself!"

Knock. Knock. Knock. The sound came from the right so he fixed his eyes there.

Nothing.

Knock. Knock. Knock. The left. Same thing—nothing.

"I don't care if you're man or child. I will kill you!" He reached upward, head woozy, and flew above the glowing silver beams to survey the entire rooftop.

Empty. Not a soul.

And no longer a sound.

He spun around, taking in the surrounding rooftops, hoping to get some clue as to who was antagonizing him. It was difficult to see into the shadows despite the red light above. But even if someone—or a group of someones—were toying with him, to hit him accurately on the roof would require sniper-like precision. It also didn't account for the foot he saw.

If that was real, he thought. Head still swimming, he got the sense the feeling would lighten up soon. He just wasn't sure how long.

Below, on the rooftop, a black ball about the size of baseball rolled to the base of the stairs before his throne.

"You're dead."

———————

"You have to stay out of this," Axiom-man had told her. The thought set Night Fowler at unease. The sky . . . it wasn't changing.

Not that it should immediately, she thought. But the idea of Axiom-man up there on Owen Tower alone, using skills newly-acquired, trying to bring down the most powerful man on the planet . . .

"I don't see a spot of blue," she whispered. "No powers." *What is he doing?*

Redsaw lowered himself near the end of Owen Tower that overlooked downtown. Below, the city was in shambles, a stark warning to the rest of the world to not come near.

But somebody had.

And they were on this roof.

When he got his hands on them, he'd use not just his powers, but every shred of combat ability he had. Whoever this was, they would be punished.

Suddenly, something firm hooked around his neck from behind and forced him to bend sideways. He lashed out with a spinning backfist only for his hand and arm to spin through the air like a helicopter blade.

The roof was empty.

As much as Redsaw wanted to clear the roof in its entirety so nothing was left unexposed, he couldn't. The throne had to stay. The beams had to stay.

The Doorway of Darkness had to stay.

A rope dart flew at him from the left. He moved, caught the rope, and gave it yank. Only the flimsy opposite end of the rope came near him, whoever had it no longer holding it.

It clicked what he was up against: Someone with martial skill. Special forces? A talented cop? Some random Joe taking matters into his own hands?

"You're running out of options," Redsaw said though he couldn't be sure of his assailant's full arsenal.

Redsaw began walking to the edge on the left. A rapid succession of what sounded like small stones hit low across the rooftop. He peered down to see what had to be a least three dozen black marbles heading straight for his feet. A step upon one before he could react sent his foot out from under him. He rose into the air a few inches and hovered so it wouldn't happen again.

He let out a blast of energy to the roof's ledge, blowing out the small barrier that separated the rooftop from a death-drop to the street tens of storeys below.

Behind him, a tap on his shoulder.

He spun around to no one.

Gritting his teeth, he'd had enough. He got into the air and did a perimeter around the building, every angle explored around the top floors and the rooftop proper.

For a brief moment, he wondered if he was dealing with a ghost or some kind of lifeform spawned from the Doorway.

He flew straight up and surveyed the roof from up high. All was stationery. Nothing moved and nothing could; all was inanimate.

As he lowered himself down, a series of small, flat circles slapped onto his body, coming from several directions. He grabbed one and yanked it off his suit, tearing a piece of fabric with it.

Every single one upon him exploded.

———

Night Fowler had to do something. Problem was, she wasn't sure she should interfere despite not fully trusting Axiom-man to do what needed to be done. Regardless of his training, the duration had been short compared to hers. The things she could do, the techniques, the physical manipulation of others, weapons—all of it, as helpful as it was, might not be required over on that rooftop.

Yet again, they might also *be* required.

There was no standing still. One could only supervise for so long before it was time to make the decision to sit it out or to act.

Night Fowler leapt off the building and used the air pockets in her wide cape to slow her descent to the ground. Once her feet touched down, she rolled with the momentum, then stood straight.

There was no work to do on the ground other than to look for then help any survivors, and she didn't think hunting and searching would be a wise use of time. She listened for sirens and shouts, some sort of indicator that help might be on the way. The air was dead quiet besides the crackling of flames and rumbling above.

She brought a finger to the side of her mask and pressed a small button. Thermo-imaging lenses slid over her eyes. She looked passed fires and heated objects for something more humanoid in shape. She glanced around every which way, hoping to locate someone she could help.

Then found something better, there, four rooftops down.

The moment the discs went off, the Doorway of Darkness roared to life and pulled Redsaw around, sucking the explosive force away from his body, sweeping the fiery blasts into the Doorway like a horizontal whirlwind. Their heat scorched his skin but an awful burn was nothing compared to what could have happened.

A shadow appeared in the air, knocked him down, then was gone.

"Enough!" Redsaw lit up his fists. "Coward! You want to face me? Then face me!"

"I have," someone said. "And I am."

Who? "Then show me."

A voice came from behind. "Hello, Redsaw."

Redsaw spun around. He . . . no, this . . . this wasn't right. And . . . no. Not possible.

And the suit was wrong.

"Axiom-man," Redsaw said, "or, at least, someone dressed sort of like him." The man before him wore Axiom-man's suit but without the cape. Dark gray and black, and his mask covered his whole head.

It couldn't be him. Axiom-man was dead.

"Close it," the man said.

Redsaw glanced up at the raw thunderous power of the Doorway of Darkness. "There is no closing it. And I'm going to kill you."

"No, I'm going to kill *you.*"

Chapter Eighteen

Night Fowler threw the grappling hook up as high as she could on the fire escape stairs alongside the building. She used the motor in her wrist gauntlet to draw herself up. Once on the top steps near the roof, she climbed the ladder and got onto the rooftop. As she slowly approached the humanoid, she pressed the button by her eyes again, withdrawing the lenses, only to see a body that was once aflame, the skin still sizzling, smoke rising from the carcass.

It was female. But why was the body up here?

The rooftop filled with dark clouds.

———

Redsaw rolled a ball of red energy from one hand to the other. "Oh, I don't think you can kill me, but if you don't mind, why don't you tell me who you really are and why you're wearing a version of that disgusting outfit."

The man in black and gray stood there, silent.

"Aren't you going to speak? Didn't you just dare to say you'll kill me."

He didn't respond.

Redsaw glanced at the ball of power in his hand then just as quickly hurled it at the man. The man dropped down, dodging it, then was back on his feet inside of a second. The man never took his eyes off him. Redsaw remained silent too, and the two did nothing but stare into each other's eyes.

I should know his voice, Redsaw thought, *but it's been a long time. And . . . this guy sounds different. Something firm behind the tone.* Strong. Redsaw huffed. A mere mortal being firm with him. Laughable. But if it *was* Axiom-man, a laugh might not be warranted. But there were no powers. No flight. No blue energy. No colorful outfit. Just . . . bravery. *Against me,* he thought. *Against me!*

Redsaw threw another energy ball at him, this time lower. The man leapt into the air, the ball of energy sweeping under him, then landed softly.

Their eyes met again.

Then a flash of bright white light went off overhead. Redsaw glanced up, temporarily blinded by its brightness. As he lowered his eyes and blinked several times to adjust back to the red hue of the rooftop, a rising swirl of gray smoke rose up from a small canister by his feet. A second later, and all was fog.

———

Night Fowler set her night-vision lenses in place over her eyes. The dark was so dense any ambient light was difficult to pick up on and amplify. The best she got was a very dark green on everything. She did a quick test and looked toward the body. The details were dull but the overall shape of the person was there. Good enough.

A dark fist popped her in the jaw from the side then two hands suddenly grabbed her and hoisted her up as if over her assailant's head. With a sharp twist, she freed herself and rolled off, dropping to the rooftop, then rolled to release the momentum before getting up and spinning on her knees, throwing two custom fire crackers to each side of Bleaken's head. The second they went off, she was on her feet and did a jumping side kick straight into his diaphragm in the hopes of knocking the wind out of him and spasming the muscle so breathing would be difficult.

If he needed to breathe, that was. She didn't know, and it didn't matter.

Night Fowler pounced on him, delivering a hard knee up and under his chin before landing and executing a front kick with the other leg, right in the sternum.

Bleaken stumbled back, holding the area. The moment she moved in again, he hid himself with a sheet of black cloud.

Immediately, Night Fowler went on guard. In her belt was a collapsible bo. She moved to grab it but a violent blow to the back of the head quickly knocked her down to the rooftop. The entire world spun, tilted left and right, moved up and down, the strong desire to let go and pass out overwhelming.

Clenching her fist, she focused and slammed her hand down on the rooftop. With her other hand, she reached for the bo. She pressed a small button toward the top end of the cylinder and the thing snapped to full extension. She spun it around the dark area while she stood, hoping one of its ends would, at minimum, tag Bleaken and give her his location.

The bo touched nothing but air.

———

Redsaw's Karate instincts kicked in and he went into full guard, ready for anything that might come his way.

A punch hit him square in the nose, breaking it. Instead of reacting, he punched out the second the impact hit and felt his fist graze a shoulder or arm. He swung out again, following the most likely path of where his target might be. The punch was blocked and Redsaw's wrist was twisted over so hard it forced him to turn with the rotation of his arm. He kicked to the side, striking this black Axiom-man in the ribs. Somewhere beyond the smoke, he heard the body roll away.

Redsaw stepped out of the gray and into the red of the rooftop. The man lay on the ground, a hand to his side.

Broken ribs. Hope it's all of them.

As he approached, about to raise a boot and stomp down on the man's head, the man extended his hand toward the ledge of the roof and grabbed something that he couldn't make out until the man rolled away and flipped over the rooftop ledge. The guy had had a rope in place. Clever. But it didn't matter. Redsaw rose into the air and went over the ledge as well, fists alight with power, ready to kill this bizarre figure the moment he spotted him, except when Redsaw hovered where the man should have been, all that remained was the loose end of the rope. Did he fall? Redsaw looked toward the ground. From this high up, it'd be difficult to discern a body on the pavement below but he had to check anyway.

A thin chain suddenly wrapped around his neck and he was pulled back toward the rooftop. With a jerk, Redsaw tore the rope attached to the chain and hovered over the roof.

The man appeared. "We aren't done."

———

There was only one option, so Night Fowler took the bo and twirled it around, each direction stabbed and struck, each time expecting to make contact, and each time making none.

There has to be a perimeter to this thing, she thought. Unless Bleaken was somewhere here in the dark expanding the area.

Her legs went out from under her. She did a break fall, slapping the bo on one side of her body against the rooftop upon impact. Her chin was tucked in so the back of her head was okay. From behind her, strong hands gripped her neck and began to squeeze. She drew the bo down and across her body before shooting it back like a rake going horizontal to vertical in a snap. A hard whack let her know she made contact. Unable to breathe, she dug one end of the bo into Bleaken's hand, and with her other hand, hit the pressure point between thumb and index finger. He had no choice but to let go as his hands lost their strength.

Night Fowler rolled backward, wrapping her legs around Bleaken's neck, and continued the roll down his back until she flipped him over entirely. He hit the rooftop with a dull thud.

As if planting a flag, she drove the bo down in between his eyes, knocking him out cold.

The black clouds on the roof remained and, she hoped, would soon dissipate.

She lay the bo across his neck and began to press down, the resistance of flesh and bone telling her that if she pushed any harder, she'd crush his windpipe and remove him as a threat for good.

Squeezing the bo hard, she pushed down . . . then stopped short just before the break.

"You should die," she grunted but as a whisper. "If you're gone, no one will be affected anymore." She held the bo hard and firm, her hands trembling as she fought against herself to go through with it. It'd be so easy. Just one violent push and he'd cease to exist.

The shallow breeze began slowly clearing the black cloud off the roof.

Trying as hard as she could, she wanted to pull the bo away but another part of her kept her in place.

"If your enemy is defeated, you need not go on," Aiyesha had once told her.

"But what if your enemy is a repeat offender?" she said, alone with him on that rooftop.

Aiyesha had never been posed the question. Night Fowler already knew the answer and it'd be nothing but a gray response. Aiyesha would tell her to do what the situation warranted, but the specifics on that . . .

Night Fowler wanted to. *Had* to . . . but held herself fast, the bo in place, the pressure applied. Not much longer and Bleaken's brain would be out of oxygen and a fatality would be imminent.

Footsteps.

She snapped her head in their direction.

"He's not worth it," the man said. Once he stepped closer within the dim light, she made out his face.

Gunn.

CHAPTER NINETEEN

IT WAS THE outfit that drove Redsaw mad. This . . . version . . . of "Axiom-man" wasn't at all who he knew and he doubted the man in black and gray before him was the real article returned from the dead.

"You wear his uniform but for the night I created," Redsaw said.

The man remained silent.

"You didn't even get the colors right, or was that intentional? Dress dark, try to intimidate me with your fancy tricks. Do you not realize you are but a mere mortal whereas I am something much more?"

"Which is?"

It would be too obvious to say "god" and that wasn't the case either. A god by comparison to a human being, yes, but not in the truest sense. "Your ruler."

The man again remained silent.

Redsaw slowly hovered around the man in a circle, looking him over from all sides, checking to see if he hid anything or was about to attempt another attack. Instead, the man stood there as calm as someone waiting to cross the street.

Redsaw flew in from behind him, heading for him to knock him down like a bowling pin. The man bent forward at the waist as Redsaw reached out . . . and missed, flying past him. He stopped, turned. The man had vanished.

"Clever but annoying," he muttered to himself. Once more he was forced to circle the rooftop to find his prey. Not this time.

This time he'd wait.

———

Night Fowler held Bleaken fast, keeping the pressure of the bo against his neck.

Gunn stood there, a mess of a man as usual, one hand in his pocket, the other pointing toward Bleaken. "You'll be cutting that star-studded loser a break if you go through with it."

"He deserves to die. You know this," she said.

"But do you?"

The words took a moment to sink in. Anger swelled within because she knew exactly what he meant. He wasn't talking physical death. He was talking something much worse. Death of a soul.

With a howl, she hurled the bo at him, the long stick spinning through the air like a helicopter blade. Gunn jumped out of the way and the bo hit the ground not far behind him, rolling along until it butted up against the interior of the roof's ledge.

"Happy now?" Gunn said, now laying on his side from the dodge.

Bleaken was still in her grasp, unconscious, and should remain that way for the next little while, but she couldn't risk him waking up. She slammed her elbow into the top of his head and let the body slump over.

Gunn got up and merely shrugged. "Beats death."

Night Fowler slowly stood and cautiously backed off from Bleaken.

The two remained silent for a short time, the city around them burning and in pieces. Up on Owen Tower, the Doorway of Darkness cast its shadowy red hue on everything, the giant Door in the sky bathing the land red as if the whole world was on fire.

Gunn glanced up in Owen Tower's direction. "We need to help your—our—friend. Got any thoughts?"

Night Fowler looked up to the tower as well. From what she could tell, Axiom-man hadn't fully engaged and she wasn't sure if he planned to. She also wasn't sure if he was even still alive. One thing to know how to fight, another to know how to use that against a superpowered opponent while you remained human. All she could do was trust he had learned enough to evade and strike and wait for the right moment to ensure Redsaw never hurt anybody again.

Never again. Not after so long of appearing then disappearing from the city's eye. No longer could the city—if it pulled out of this—endure a boogeyman just waiting for the right moment to come out of the darkness and destroy, then retreat back into it.

"We need to get up there," she said.

"Pretty sure the elevator ain't working," Gunn said.

"Then we take the stairs, you idiot," she said, looking him square in the face. She walked past him.

From behind her, she heard Gunn mutter, "You didn't even tell me your name."

You don't need to know.

———

Redsaw waited. It could have been a few minutes or twenty. He was not finished with the Doorway of Darkness and this . . . distraction . . . impeded his progress. However, he didn't want to get back to work without dealing with this Axiom-man wannabe.

A loud *ping* rang out somewhere near the silver spires. A random noise or intentional?

Intentional.

Redsaw didn't move toward the beams but watched them closely.

Another *ping*.

He engaged a keener view.

Silence.

No one.

Two light smacks struck his heels just below the ankles. He brushed his cape to the side to have a look and . . . was that mud? Did the guy just throw mud at him?

A split second later, the mud exploded and Redsaw screamed as his heels were blown off his feet, removing them entirely. Blood poured from the areas not cauterized from the flame. He dropped to the rooftop on a slower decent then grabbed the spot where his heels once were. Even through his gloves he caught the texture of charred flesh and slick strings of flesh. He fired up his hands and growled loud as he used the heat to seal the wounds. He expected nothing but sharp, lingering pain afterward but instead found his feet numb. Either the nerves were fried or he was in shock.

Before he could shout at his invisible opponent, the man was somehow flying at an angle through the air, foot drawn and about to plant hard. A violent jumping side kick ripped across Redsaw's face and he hit the rooftop in a daze.

He blasted out streaks of red energy in retaliation but couldn't land anything on his target because . . . his target was gone again.

Gathering himself, he rose into the air. "I will tear this place apart!" But he knew he couldn't. Not after what he had created. Any damage to the Doorway would risk everything.

Redsaw dropped down hard onto the rooftop, keeping his weight more on the balls of his feet so as to not aggravate what was left of the back of them. Each step was slow, careful. He held up his guard. If this guy insisted on a fistfight, a fiery fistfight he shall have.

———

Getting in the building and onto the main floor of Owen Tower was a bit of a climb over broken-up pavement and chunks of rubble. The entire lobby was desolate and covered in fine gray dust from all the chaos. Then the building shook.

Now, in the stairwell, throat and mouth dry, legs starting to fatigue, Gunn glanced at the upcoming door at the next floor.

Twenty.

Nice even number.

Nice terrible reminder there were at least another twenty to go, if not more, before they reached their destination. What made it worse was this person in gray was moving at a good clip, taking the stairs two at a time as if they did this march every day. They were somewhere above . . . he hoped. No sound came from the stairs but it wouldn't surprise him if this person snuck up behind him quietly.

He stopped for a moment and put his hands on his knees. *Disgraceful,* he thought of his own feeble efforts to climb a mere set of stairs.

No, not a *set* of stairs.

Twenty sets.

And at least twenty more to go.

Gunn swallowed back the urge to puke and kept going.

———

A quick kick to the face from somewhere out of his line of sight caught Redsaw off guard and he stumbled back. He lashed out with a couple punches of his own only to strike mere air. He'd taken strikes by Axiom-man before. This strike . . . there wasn't the same amount of power behind it. It was merely human. It hurt . . . but it was a human punch.

This guy wasn't Axiom-man, just someone, it seemed, who was carrying the torch. No matter. Once he finally got hold of him, it'd be as simple as grabbing either end of the man's body and ripping him in two. Or, maybe, a simple punch to the face as hard as possible to punch straight through it and leave nothing but a gaping hole in the skull.

Redsaw's feet went out from under him and his back hit the rooftop hard. A heel came down on the nose of his cowl, breaking the mask and cracking the nose beneath. Blood spilled out and leaked to either side, running down his cheeks.

With a roar, Redsaw righted himself and used his flight to get vertical. The sensation of blood running down his face excited him and he wasn't sure why.

For a fleeting moment, a strange thought came to him: *I grow stronger with each kill. What would happen if I killed myself? Death . . . or . . . a release of all I've harnessed?* No. Too much of a chance to take and this was not the time to even ponder the idea.

A kick to the stomach doubled him over. He struck out with a backfist and clipped what felt like bone, possibly a chin. Then he heard a body skid across the rooftop.

It took a moment to locate the wannabe but there he was, about fifteen feet off to the side, face down.

Redsaw hovered over and powered up his fists. *End him.* He shot forth. The body rolled to the side the moment the blast of his beams hit the rooftop and tore it up, leaving a hole to the floor below. Debris fell like rain, dust like steam.

A series of flashing strobe lights materialized in the dust cloud, their bright white flashing flares stealing Redsaw's vision. In an instant, a chain wrapped around his neck from behind and the force of the man's weight pulled Redsaw to the ground. He grimaced when the rear of his feet touched the rooftop and a shot of pain ripped through them and up his legs. Redsaw jumped into the air, spun around, and flew at the man, pinning him to the rooftop. Redsaw grasped the chain around his neck and tore it off, the links raining to the ground.

The heat coming off Redsaw's wrists started to cook through the man's simple outfit.

Somehow, the man in black and gray got his leg free and brought it around Redsaw's neck, jerking him over and down sideways, a sudden leg lock around Redsaw's neck.

Strangely, the first thing Redsaw thought was how the man didn't make a sound as the fabric on the shoulders burned away. Anybody else would have screeched and howled.

Now in a choke hold between the man's legs, Redsaw went to slam his fist into the man's shin to break it. But the man released the moment the fist came in, leg quickly absent, Redsaw hitting only the air. But the other leg was still on the other side of his neck. He aimed his fist but the leg slipped out before he could land the blow.

A punch to his temple sent a blaze of pain across his eyes, doubling up the impact of discomfort as the strobe lights still flashed.

He struck out, aiming to hit anything—any*one*—around him but to no avail.

Above, the Doorway over the land rumbled with thunder and flashes of red lightning skipped and crackled through the sky.

That was either the Doorway or . . . my master. He can't be happy. I'm *not* happy. "No more," he grunted and got himself upright yet again. "We are done!"

"Then come and get me," the man said.

Redsaw followed the voice then squinted because of the strobes.

The man stood facing him, directly in front of the Doorway of Darkness.

As Redsaw hovered, he sent blast after blast to the rooftop behind him, slowly but surely taking out the strobe lights one by one. When the last one went out, momentary darkness stole his vision before his eyes adjusted to the sweet glow of red.

Redsaw lowered himself, facing the man, his feet slightly off the ground.

Fists aglow with power and rage, the man in front of him was a clear shot. He didn't bother with words.

Just action.

The second before he discharged his hands at him, this "Axiom-man" hopped backward and went through the Doorway.

CHAPTER TWENTY

THE STAIRWELL CAME to an end about fifty feet below the rooftop, the remaining stairs destroyed without even so much as their leftover rubble sticking out of the supporting wall. High above, a jagged hole revealed the red-and-black-clouded sky.

Gunn's wheezing ragged on Night Fowler's ears. *He's a cop, for crying out loud. No standard for being in shape?*

"Draw your weapon," she told him, "and stay here. If anything red comes through that opening, shoot it."

"Since when" —Gunn coughed then spat— "do you give me orders?"

She fired her grappling hook to the opening on the roof. Before she let it take her up, she said, "Since the world is about to end."

Gunn's eyes widened and, it seemed, it finally sunk in. If Redsaw wasn't stopped now, there wouldn't be a second chance. He nodded and drew his weapon.

She glanced at it, then at him, then rode the line up.

––––––––––

Redsaw did not enter. Instead, he hovered there, mouth agape, wondering how in the hell someone would dare attempt entering the Doorway of Darkness. A mere human no less! The forces within the Doorway would tear a human being apart.

Suicide. Wise choice, he thought. But why would this man fight him only to kill himself? Unless the man felt he had done what he could and knew either Redsaw would end his life or he would.

He wasn't sure if he should enter to confirm the kill. And since the realm was an endless void of red and black clouds, locating the man's body—if a body remained—would be near impossible.

Without warning, the Doorway of Darkness shook, crackles of red energy spewing out from its frame, connecting with the silver beams then retreated back in. The entirety of Owen Tower rocked. Above, thunder boomed over and over, each bang louder than the last.

Redsaw covered his ears when the force of the sound blew out the windows of the remaining downtown buildings.

His tower. His beacon of strength and might and display of lordship shook and quaked.

What the hell was happening?

He took off into the Doorway and frantically searched the void for any sign of the man.

Nothing.

But something was different. This place held strength and security, a density you could feel. That was lighter now, more fragile. Or so it seemed.

He spun around, searching this way and that, wondering what caused the disturbance.

"Get him out!" his master shouted, the sound of his thundering voice coming from all directions.

"Get him!"

Redsaw froze.

A bright blue light shone atop the black of his cape from behind and over his shoulders.

———

The line had cut off when the building shook and Night Fowler had attempted to get onto the roof. She fell back through the hole, scanning for Gunn on her way down.

She didn't see him.

Quickly, she threw out her cape and caught what air she could in the narrow space to slow her decent onto something that would hurt on impact but at least wouldn't kill her. She struck a set of stairs and tumbled down. When the descent didn't stop, she folded herself into a roll to avoid as much injury as possible.

Night Fowler slammed up against one of the stairwell's walls, the shock of the impact shooting the air out of her lungs and stealing her breath. She did her best to relax herself so eventually slow and small sips of air would enter her lungs before she could resume breathing normally. She tipped onto her side, her head landing near the edge of where the stairwell revealed an open gape to the floors below. Mixed in behind a veil of dust, she saw a body laying on a set of steps below.

Gunn.

He didn't move.

Redsaw moved like lightning and spun around with a violent hook punch.

Axiom-man caught his fist dead on, his fingers wrapped around Redsaw's hand, and squeezed.

Redsaw froze and Axiom-man caught the glimmer of his blue power in his enemy's eye. His suit, still black and gray, was awash in blue light from his glowing eyes, a halo around each, powered to the max.

Axiom-man shoved Redsaw's fist back at him and then came in hard with a direct punch to Redsaw's sternum, sending the man in the black cape flying backward into the void. Launching his flight, Axiom-man sped toward him, fist cocked, ready to deliver a devastating blow to Redsaw's head.

Redsaw blew out a surge of energy from his hands as a counter but Axiom-man flew at him anyway, twirling through and around the beams of red energy and heading straight for his target. Another shot connected square across Redsaw's jaw. As his fist finished the motion, Axiom-man caught note the impact point sent Redsaw's jaw slightly off its hinge. He used the pain to his advantage and came in with a straight punch to Redsaw's neck before kicking him hard farther into the void. Where the Doorway was right now, it didn't matter. All that mattered was putting an end to Redsaw once and for all.

Axiom-man threw out both fists in front of him and kicked on the speed as fast as he could, pile-driving himself directly into Redsaw's ribcage. His shot connected, lingered, and enabled him to push Redsaw farther and farther away from any hope of escape from this place . . . even if it meant no escape for himself.

As the two ripped through the void at what Axiom-man estimated was around two hundred kilometers an hour, Redsaw tried to speak but couldn't seem to find the words.

Axiom-man flipped himself backward and extended his legs in a double kick to Redsaw's middle, sending the man in black and red even further into the murk.

He kept on him. Never let up. Overwhelm your opponent. Disorient them. Frustrate them.

Eyes alit with blue crackling power, Axiom-man let the energy build and build until all he saw was bright blue, so bright it was near white. He tried to peer through the light, to see Redsaw on the other side, but his powers forbade him. It was either charge up and go in blind or charge down so he could see past the glare.

Turning his attention inward, Axiom-man focused on sensing Redsaw's presence, wrestling back the sick feeling their two opposing power sets triggered within him. He turned his head slightly to the right and let loose, blasting a steady stream of blue energy into Redsaw. Only when the light pouring out of his eyes dimmed did he see Redsaw with his arms crossed in front him, alight with red power, taking in the blow.

Axiom-man didn't let up.

Night Fowler crouched down beside Gunn's body. The old fool. This was not his fight even though she was aware he viewed it as such. Now he lay there, bloody and . . . dead?

She leaned in and put a hand on his chest. His breath was so shallow and weak, she couldn't make out any air going in or out of his lungs through the fabric of her mask, but her hand slightly rising and falling indicated he was breathing.

For how long, she couldn't be sure.

She glanced up. That's where the fight was. That's where it all rested and, after it was over, where humanity's fate lay as well. She looked to Gunn then back up at the hole in the roof then back to Gunn again.

"One life or many?" she said softly. The logic was obvious; the doing was not. She had to save Gunn *and* help save everybody else. *You do what is immediate in battle. What's in front of you is what it is and needs doing.* She furrowed her brow. *If he stops breathing, I am* not *giving him mouth-to-mouth.*

————

Axiom-man kept on, fighting back against Redsaw's resistance to his power. The second he was in range, Axiom-man slammed his foot through Redsaw's guard and delivered a heel to the man's collarbone, still pouring on the blue energetic heat. Redsaw immediately grasped the spot, his power loosening. Axiom-man twisted and sent another kick toward Redsaw's head. Redsaw deflected it.

A violent blast of red power to Axiom-man's stomach caused his insides to cave in despite the thin aura of blue light of protection shining over his body.

Though Redsaw was a good hundred feet away, Axiom-man heard him clearly: "I will *not* fight a ghost!"

"Even one that fights back?" Axiom-man said, though he wasn't sure if his voice carried in this place the same as Redsaw's.

"It's . . . it's this place. You . . . you were here then . . . gone. Dead. You did not remain!"

Assuming Redsaw's thoughts were scattered, Axiom-man flew directly at him, digging in hard and going as fast as he could. He twisted his body into a flying side kick and struck Redsaw in the chest like a battering ram. Redsaw flew back head over heels, tumbling over and over before he finally ceased and just hovered in the air, limp, seemingly beaten or unconscious.

But Axiom-man knew better. *Never fall for your opponent's tricks. Never believe what you see. Only believe what you've done.*

He knew what he needed to do. If it worked—the thought sickened him but he knew it was the only way. Rocketing toward him, Axiom-man flew past but grabbed

Redsaw's cape, then spun around in the air and brought it back around so it looped around Redsaw's neck. He went around twice for good measure then hauled the man up as if stringing along someone on a noose, except here there was no gravity so he'd compensate the material's strain on the neck by flying faster, creating tension in the cape and ensuring he cut off Redsaw's air supply.

Axiom-man gave the black cape a violent tug, hoping to crack the neck.

Redsaw stirred.

CHAPTER TWENTY-ONE

THE DROP IN the stairwell of Owen Tower was at least thirty floors, if not more. The stairs themselves were mostly destroyed or destroyed beyond use. Only small juts of concrete stair stuck out here and there in the crimson spiral downward that faded into darkness.

Night Fowler had no way to carry Gunn down. She thought if maybe an elevator was working and if she could find a door to one of the floors and give it a try, there could be a chance. *And if they are working and something goes wrong?* She couldn't leave him here and, once again, was tempted to sacrifice him if it meant the salvation of many but remembered that was not her call to make. Not here, not now.

Not for this.

She had to trust her ally and hope he had things under control.

Or as close to it as possible.

But that didn't help her right now. What mattered was getting Gunn to safety and then seeing what could be done if the fight above their heads was still occurring.

She felt along her belt and found her grappling hook. Thirty floors or more meant over three hundred feet of line, which she didn't have. No one did. The bulk of carrying around that much line would be impractical. She'd have to go fifty or so feet at a time for what she had in mind. First job was to secure Gunn, and with that man's big belly and bulky, awkward clothing, who knew how much line it would take for even that?

"This sucks," she said and got to work.

———

A fiery blast of red energy shot past Axiom-man just as he moved his shoulder out of the way. He stomped down hard on top of Redsaw's head, hoping to compress the spine and create a tremor of pain through his body.

Redsaw went limp again.

Axiom-man drew the body up by the cape as if hauling in a catch pull by pull. He wrapped his fingers around Redsaw's neck and held him aloft over the void below.

"All this time. All those lives. And you kept getting away and away and away," Axiom-man said. "There will be no more getting away. Never again." He reached for Redsaw's cowl and got a couple fingers under the band beneath the eyes. As he moved the mask up, he wondered who lurked beneath the disguise, the coward who hid while he killed.

He removed the mask to see a man with black eyes, bruises, and sweaty black hair. The face was damaged from the fight, puffy and swollen in places, distorting the man's true visage. There was a familiarity to the face but with one eye near swollen shut and the other a mess of red and purple, the damage was a mask on its own.

Quickly, Axiom-man's wrist was snatched and locked tight in Redsaw's grip as he came to. Growling, Redsaw tore the mask from Axiom-man's hand and delivered a red energy-laced punch right between Axiom-man's eyes. Axiom-man's world flipped backwards and upside down.

The cape! Did he still hold . . . the . . . . His hand was empty when he glanced down and Redsaw was nowhere to be seen.

Axiom-man scanned all around, hoping to catch a glimpse of him only to be met with the sight of red and black clouds, the perfect backdrop for Redsaw to disappear into.

His heart picked up pace, dreading the thought of having to start all over again. *No, not starting over: Continuing. Your opponent might return from the pain with only the mind to destroy you.* They were Aiyesha's words, not his, but were a warning. Sometimes the seemingly defeated came back stronger.

Like him, in a way. Came back with the skills needed to defea—

A pile drive blast drove into Axiom-man's back, the blue aura over him shuddering top to bottom from the explosion of red power.

Redsaw floated down in front of him. "Like you said, we aren't done."

———

Thank goodness part of martial arts was the use of physics and geometry. Night Fowler had Gunn wrapped up and now had his limp body dangling over the hole once occupied with stairs. She was in a quasi-Judo-throw position, her line over her shoulder, facing the opposite direction and using her own center of mass to control Gunn's weight so his bulky frame wouldn't topple her over and throw her down into the hole with him.

Carefully, she altered her stance and slowly turned herself around, Gunn still stable.

It would take a long time to get to the bottom, and that was assuming once at the bottom, their exit wasn't blocked off by rubble and debris. She'd do her best to try and catch sight of an obstruction as she descended so she could alter her plan if needed instead of wasting time.

She let Gunn down inch by inch.

Above, the Doorway of Darkness crackled and boomed on the rooftop.

———

The wave of nausea hit Axiom-man hard, going from zero to a hundred in a split second. His brain on a tilt-a-whirl, his body collapsing inward from the extreme sickness that struck him all at once, all he could do was try to right himself.

Should I retreat and regroup? he wondered. *Possible, maybe, but he'd be right on my tail and . . . and . . . .* The swarm of dizziness removed all thought and all he recognized was a man in a black and red suit, black cape, and a black cowl awkwardly sitting on his head and covering what looked like a mutated face swollen with damage.

The sickness forced Axiom-man's body to tremble and a burst of sweat coated his skin. He could only suppose this time, now that he had the aura, it took longer for Redsaw's presence to upset his physiology never mind the damage this place was doing simply by being in its atmosphere. He had to get out, had to find a way to recharge otherwise . . . he could die here.

He needed the Doorway out. He glanced around, stomach lurching, fighting the urge to throw up, most of his energy spent trying to swallow it back down.

A violent whoomph struck the side of his head and sent him reeling backward into the void.

"Pay attention." All he could manage was to mouth the words but he meant them all the same.

A dark shadow came in from the left. Axiom-man flew sideways toward it, caught Redsaw's outstretched arm and quickly pulled, then threw the man downwards into the void.

Vision blurry, it was difficult to discern him from the red and black clouds all around.

I need out, he thought.

He glanced around again, searching for some sort of outline of crackling energy that would indicate the Doorway.

The sickness spinning his world and forcing a deep heaviness on his eyes, Axiom-man realized he only had one choice if he was going to survive this.

Just one.

He *shifted* and turned his powers off.

———

As impossible as it was, Redsaw accepted the fact this was indeed Axiom-man somehow returned from the dead. Accepted what seemed like two years of freedom without his interference was now over and, if that freedom was to be regained, he had to do what he did before and that was end him.

Permanently.

Redsaw scanned the clouds and tried to sense Axiom-man's presence to pinpoint his location and attack.

There was . . . nothing.

———

Axiom-man glanced over his shoulder to the thick black cloud far in the distance. Though he couldn't be sure, he hoped its backdrop would help hide his dark suit and keep him out of sight, at least for a while. Right now, all he could manage was catching his breath, no different than getting it together after the torrential outpour of emptying one's guts in a bucket. But it was in this state that he felt every ounce of pain Redsaw had dished, each shot and blast turning his body into a useless lump of limp dough.

I'll recover, he thought. *I hope.* He had to get out of here. The idea had been to trap Redsaw inside this realm, lock him away, and somehow close the Doorway of Darkness. But, he realized, that was impossible now. Not with it opened atop and across the entire province, if not farther. "I have no idea how to close it," he said quietly. "I can't zipper it shut like last time. It's too big. It's too—" But what if he sealed just the Doorway? Would it shut off everything in the sky because of the cut-off of the source point? But there had to be another source point for it to branch out like that, but a second Doorway? Was it possible? He didn't know. He had only encountered one and that was a long time ago and the cause of everything terrible that had happened to him, the city, and . . . Valerie.

Tears pinched at the corners of his eyes at her memory. He had hoped to leave her out of his head coming here, engaging in this battle, focusing solely on the task at hand. He had left himself behind and went deep into this newfound warrior side of himself. Keep emotions out of it. Be practical. Think things through. But that was never the case with the heart. The heart eventually came out and won every time. He wanted to say he'd finish this for her, get her retribution and justice. And, yeah, that'd be part of it, but this whole thing couldn't just be about her. If Redsaw was left unchecked, undefeated—the world would pay.

I need help. "I need help." He wanted the messenger to hear him, to come to his aid, to give him what he needed to finally—oh so finally—put an end to Redsaw and his reign of terror. But that wasn't part of the deal. This moment, this fight, was why he had received his gifts, why he had become Axiom-man, and why he had to finish it being Axiom-man.

But right now? Gabriel felt lost in a dense forest of forever with no way out.

CHAPTER TWENTY-TWO

"HEY! WHAT? WHOA!" Gunn shrieked below.

"Finally," Night Fowler said. *Welcome back, you fat slob.*

"Hey, who's up there?"

"Me," she said.

"What?"

"I said me!"

"What's going on? Why am I tied up?"

"Because I'm saving your life."

There was a mutter but she couldn't make it out. Maybe with Gunn awake, they could form a better plan or, ideally, maybe she could untie him and then get to the roof to see what she could do to help.

The line violently jerked outward and Gunn's howls sounded below. Night Fowler pulled it back. "Stop moving!"

"But . . ."

"Stop!"

"Okay, okay!"

Night Fowler strained as she took her end of the line and pressed it against a jut of concrete that was once a stair sticking out of the wall, then as quickly as possible, so as to not lose grip, pulled out a small black spray can. She sprayed it over her line, coating it with a gray foam as it lay against the busted stair. She silently counted to ten then pulled her hand back from the line. The foam was dry and rock solid, cementing the line to the broken stair. She turned, gripped the line that led down to Gunn, and descended it like a fire pole.

Without his powers activated, Axiom-man couldn't move around within the void. He needed flight for that. He quickly flashed back to getting Redsaw's attention which had summoned him here. He had turned his powers on in the void, disrupting the atmosphere. But it was the voice that said, "Intruder," that got him to quickly get out and power down. Who or what was that? It wasn't Redsaw. It was someone else and he wasn't sure if it was a *who* or a *what*.

He needed out and there was no Doorway. He eyed the clouds around him, attempting to check for movement. There was drifting, but it could all be an optical illusion if it was merely the clouds moving.

Screams of frustration and rage sounded in the distance, seeming to come from everywhere and difficult to pinpoint. If Redsaw came near, he'd have to activate his powers again to fight. If there was a surface to stand on in here, then he might not have to, but with his feet touching nothing but murky red and black cloudy air, any technique that required a grounding point couldn't be used.

Arms out before him, he attempted to breaststroke through the air to see if movement was possible or not. He couldn't tell if he was moving or if there was a mild breeze in this place.

He stopped, glanced around for Redsaw.

So far, he seemed safe.

He then checked for the Doorway but no success.

There had to be a way out.

———

Axiom-man was in here somewhere, Redsaw knew, but why he couldn't detect him, he wasn't sure. He scanned the clouds and hated that Axiom-man's dark suit hid him amongst the billowing mists. Redsaw squinted and peered carefully where black might be on black, hoping the dark gray portions of Axiom-man's suit would assist in making him stand out, or stand out enough to get a location.

"Where is he?" Redsaw said, the question intended for his master.

"Not where," his master said. "What."

———

Red lightning snapped and cracked around Axiom-man. He twisted and turned to the left or right on instinct as the streaks of red fire struck close to him but still had no chance of touching him.

"Maybe not for long," Axiom-man said. "I could be a lightning rod in here so far as I know."

Thunder sounded on the right and only the right, a long, droning rumble that ended in a violent crash.

Then all went silent except for the crackle of streaks of red lightning.

The thunder returned, still on the right. Rumble. Build. Bang!

Then quiet again.

The cycle repeated several times and Axiom-man wondered if he had moved because this particular kind of thunder wasn't sounding before. It was either that or the thunder decided to manifest not far off to the right. What it meant, if anything, he wasn't sure. In the meantime, he waited for the next boom.

Floor thirteen.

Fitting.

As if more could go wrong today. It didn't matter, Night Fowler decided. *It's just a number.* And it was the only floor thus far with enough of a concrete outcrop near a barricaded door to hold them both.

Once Gunn was untied, he rolled onto his hands and knees and caught his breath as if he'd just run a marathon.

Night Fowler was already at work clearing the door. Thankfully, as sad as it was, her voice modulator masked she was female. She couldn't see Gunn taking orders from a lady. Not a machoistic bum like him. His love of justice was his only redeeming quality.

He joined her, grabbing chunks of concrete and broken stairwell rail and throwing them into the stairwell so they could attempt to pry open the door. Once clear, he yanked at the handle as if to throw it open only to be stuck fighting with it.

"Stupid, fluffin' . . ."

Fluffin'? she thought. She batted his hand out of the way and produced a small piece of putty wrapped in cellophane from her belt. She pulled the cellophane off and pushed the putty into the crack where the latch was. A press of a button on a small device and a small boom burst from the site along with smoke and the smell of scorched metal.

She pulled the door open.

Gunn looked at her, raised an eyebrow. Then finally said, "After you," and gestured toward the door.

The blast came in hot and fast and nailed Axiom-man in the side. The sheer heat of Redsaw's energy beams seared his outfit despite it being flame-retardant. His skin and muscles stung beneath the fabric and, on instinct, he *shifted*, power flooding through his system and immediately giving him control over his body floating in the clouds. Axiom-man fired up his eyes to shoot back but couldn't see Redsaw anywhere except . . . the wave of nausea began to grow which meant—

Redsaw came in from below, scooping his hands under Axiom-man's arm pits and taking him straight up into a cluster of bright and dark red clouds.

Thunder rumbled and crashed and more streaks of red lightning blasted horizontally beside him.

Axiom-man brought two knife-hand strikes down onto Redsaw's trapezius muscles, Charlie-horsing them in the hopes the man would let go.

With a grunt on impact, Redsaw clocked Axiom-man across the jaw. Axiom-man fired back, hitting Redsaw between the eyes. The man in black and red's head lolled back . . . then slowly set itself forward. Axiom-man kneed him hard in the gut then brought an elbow across Redsaw's temple that should have knocked him out but instead only seemed to fuel his rage.

Redsaw's fists lit in fiery fury, the power scorching through Axiom-man's suit. He sent a blast from his eyebeams down on his enemy, forcing him loose and sending him flying back.

With a growl, Redsaw flew at him fast. Axiom-man sent off another blast and Redsaw deflected it with a blast of his own.

More rumbling. Another thunder crash.

Those streaks of lightning were getting closer. Axiom-man could not get caught up in that storm.

Redsaw grabbed him and threw him through the air, ever closer to the roaring storm. The sound of thunder crashed in his ears and banged so hard in his head all thought vanished for a moment. He forgot where he was when his body rocked from the soundwaves but shook off the confusion. Redsaw must have felt it too because he briefly stopped midair then progressed toward him.

Axiom-man hooked a punch from the left then the right then the left then the right, beating Redsaw's head without mercy only to marvel how well the man took each blow despite him clearly being caught up in the beating.

So much strength, Axiom-man thought. *Definitely not the same guy from before. Those years with the Doorway of Darkness . . . did they power him, strengthen him, turn him into something unstoppable?* His heart ached at the thought and so did the concern in his gut. He dropped an elbow on top of Redsaw's head, knocking the man lower. Redsaw drew his fists together and blasted Axiom-man's way, sending him tumbling head over heels through the void.

Thunder banged and crashed, the shockwave from the sound forcing every muscle and bone in Axiom-man's body to tremor.

Red lighting streaked nearby.

Redsaw flew in hard, fists out before him, a stream of red energy headed in Axiom-man's direction. Axiom-man blasted at the beams with his eyes and a violent and bright clash of purple burst the second the beams connected. It was difficult to see past the energy impact point but it appeared Redsaw had steered the merger out of the way and into . . .

Another snap of bright red lightning and Axiom-man swore he felt his eyeballs jerk from their spots in their sockets as the purple beam caught the red and the red yanked him from his position and jerked him along its current.

CHAPTER TWENTY-THREE

THE POWER WAS out on the thirteenth floor but the window at the end of the hall let in a little of the dark red light from outside.

Gunn produced his firearm.

All Night Fowler had to do was look at him.

"What? Not all of us have ultra powers," he said.

Don't let on that you don't, she thought. "Let's go."

"Where?"

She pointed to the other end of the hall.

"More stairs?"

"Might be intact."

Gunn glanced over to the elevators off to the side in the middle of the hallway then glanced back to the stairs at the opposite end.

They moved down the hall and Gunn pressed both elevator buttons as they passed. Night Fowler stopped but didn't turn around. She heard his footsteps continue behind her.

"Nothin'," he said.

She continued. *Obviously.*

The door leading into the other stairwell opened with ease. A good sign. They entered the dark of the stairwell. Not even the small emergency lights or exit signs were alit. She pulled out a flashlight and aimed the beam at the stairs leading down to the twelfth floor.

Gunn held his weapon aloft. "Let me go ahead."

She stopped him with a palm to his shoulder. "Let me."

Axiom-man spun and twisted with the violent current of electrical red energy as it streaked across the sky, his only link to it the beams coming out of his eyes that began ripping them from his face. He cut the power only to find out he was too late and beam after beam struck him and sent him tumbling as if he was a chosen swimmer in its current and it was helping him along.

Another blast sent him reeling and for a moment everything went dark only to be awakened a moment later with a thunderous boom that rocked him to his core and sent his ears ringing.

He tried to fly out of the current only to be brought back by another blast of red lightning. Head spinning, stomach churning, all he could do was center himself and roll with it as he was taught.

"If there is not an opening for an attack, you make one," Aiyesha had said. Part of the lesson was also learning how to time making one, which sometimes meant you rolled with the blows until an opportunity for movement and space or an offense presented itself.

He took another blast, regretting it a split second later. It felt like his powers had been completely stolen from him and it was only a small charge of blue light he brought to his eyes that confirmed otherwise.

Thunder slammed in the clouds.

Red lightning.

A crackling frame.

An open Doorway.

Redsaw flew along the thundering clouds and horizontal streaks of lightning to try and track

Axiom-man down. All he knew was Axiom-man got caught up in the storm and vanished. Whether he was alive or dead had to be confirmed.

I have to be careful, he thought. *If indeed it is him, he somehow survived what happened and somehow made his way back from the dead. In the currency he and I deal in, that means he could be more powerful than he's letting on.*

There was only one option when, not *if*, he found him: No mercy.

———

Axiom-man took another hit of red lightning and he immediately gagged on the little that he had in his stomach that suddenly decided to show up in his throat. He hated swallowing it back and winced as the sharp citrusy foul went back down to his stomach. He tumbled through the air, trying his best to aim himself toward that Doorway.

Lightning struck him again, his limbs went numb, and nothing but sand filled his head. In the haze that was his vision, he aimed for the Doorway as he tumbled through the air, using his flight to steer until he was . . . was . . . out!

The red and black clouds vanished from sight and Axiom-man hit a series of boulders as he tumbled down a rocky hill. Gravity fully in charge, he raced toward a massive stone jutting out of the hill. Impact would break every bone in his body. Quickly, he flew up and over in his chaotic tumble and landed hard on the other side, continuing his decent down the hill. Finally, he hit a slope of grass and friction began to take over. Sky over ground, sky over ground, sky over—he rolled along the ground until the inertia finally dissipated. Just to lie still for a moment, face to the grass, the night all around him, soothed the chaos within.

"Get up," he said. "Nap later." It seemed every muscle objected to his effort to stand but he made his body obey him anyway. At least out here, away from that place, he would be stronger. He just needed a moment to regather.

Somewhere not too far away: "Who do ya suppose that is?" Male. Gruff.

"I don't know." Female. Familiar.

"He came from that there hole there," the man said.

"Then I doubt he's our friend," she said.

Axiom-man realized who was approaching. He thought he had dealt with them over two years ago, but a lot could also change in two years. He *shifted* and powered down. He'd call upon his powers if needed. Right now, maybe he could fool them into thinking he was someone else. After all, Battle Bruiser wasn't very bright.

He got to his feet, allowed a swoon of disorientation to wash over him, and let it lift. A big breath of fresh air and a slow exhale.

Axiom-man raised his hands into a fighting guard and welcomed their approach.

———

The door to floor twelve didn't open. Neither did the door to floor eleven, and Night Fowler didn't want to waste the explosives in her belt in case she needed them for something more important later.

She shined the flashlight down the remaining flights. The powerful beam nearly reached the ground floor, but not enough to reveal what was at the bottom.

"Any grand plans?" Gunn asked.

She looked at him. "Get out of this stairwell with you." She moved past him. "You're slowing me down."

Night Fowler didn't need to look back to know Gunn frowned.

———

Battle Bruiser came in with a wide right hook then stopped his fist about halfway and pulled it back. "Oh dang," he said. "Lady, you gotta see this!"

Axiom-man took the opportunity of distraction and jumped into the air and sent a flying side kick right between Bruiser's eyes. The big man stumbled back, dazed.

"Hey!" Lady Fire said and let out a stream of flame in Axiom-man's direction.

Axiom-man dove to the ground, rolled, got back to his feet, and threw two metal stars in her direction, one striking each of her hands.

She grabbed one then the other. "Ow!" The star blades protruded from the top of each hand. He could only hope they severed a tendon or two to make hand use difficult. She could still use her flames, he knew, but maybe the cuts would make doing so more painful. It was difficult to say. He didn't fully understand each of their power sets. Just what they could do . . . so took a mental note to keep that kind of item in mind in the future.

Bruiser seemed to have stabled himself and charged at Axiom-man headlong. The big man came in too hot and fast for a counter. Axiom-man leapt into the air just as he was about to connect, but the tips of his toes caught Bruiser's back, forcing him to somersault in the air, roll to the ground, slow himself, turn, and launch back. Battle Bruiser stormed up to him and let loose a left and a right. Axiom-man ducked each blow then slammed his fists into either side of Bruiser's body, nailing the floating ribs as hard as he could. The man was dense, thick with more layers of muscle than seemed humanly possible. Punching him was like punching a packed, canvas sandbag. Some give but mostly solid. Axiom-man ripped in twice more before being forced back by a push and then a hard shot to the mouth. His lips split beneath his mask and the warmth of blood quickly flowed down his chin while the taste of copper flooded over his tongue. His mask absorbed some of the blood, but there was so much he had to pull back, tug open the bottom of his mask, and spit the blood out of his mouth.

Everything from his nose down to his chin was numb from the blow and the horrible uncomfortable feeling of two fat lips made him grimace. He reasserted his mask.

Lady Fire sent a ring of flame around him, lighting up the dry grass and locking him in this circle of fire with the two of them.

"Why did you change colors?" Lady Fire asked.

Strange question. Axiom-man didn't respond. On purpose. Let them guess.

"You're dead-man, not Ax—"

"Shh!" Lady Fire told Bruiser. "Name's off limits, remember?"

"Right." Bruiser snorted up a ball of phlegm then spat it out. "He looks more like a guy tryin' to be him but I think this dude is color blind."

"Is that true?" Lady Fire said to Axiom-man. "Are you color blind?"

Axiom-man quickly scanned the fiery ring for an opening but found none. He was a sheep in the pen with the wolves closing in.

"Roast him," Bruiser said.

"Gladly," she said and raised her arms.

Axiom-man moved in and feigned a deliberately wide and exaggerated crescent kick. Her eyes darted toward the incoming. He pulled the kick by planting the foot down and then drew himself forward, the feint enough to close the gap. The second his foot touched down, he was within range of a backfist to her cheekbone. He cranked her as hard as he could.

"Hey!" Bruiser shouted and came at him, but before the big man could grab hold, Axiom-man took Lady Fire's daze as a chance to grab one arm by the wrist, the other hand used to spin her body and hurl her toward the ring of flame. She fell partly inside it. With a wild shriek, she moved to get out but her wings caught fire and she tipped forward.

A flash of white burst before him then vanished. Everything went black. Then the sensation of the ground beneath him and a wild headache that forced him to squint. Had Bruiser nailed him any lower, the man would have connected bang-on with his temple and would have most likely ended him.

Ears ringing, the inside of his head heavy with a brick for a brain, Axiom-man did his best to stand.

Lady Fire screamed as she burst forth from the flames. Instinct took over and Axiom-man's leg impulsively thrust out and he sent her back into the fire. Out of his peripheral, Bruiser went to grab him. Axiom-man dropped low and delivered a fist to each of the insides of Bruiser's knees, then did the same to either side of his groin before striking him right in every man's bullseye.

Battle Bruiser's legs collapsed under him and his hands clutched between his legs, making his head completely vulnerable. Axiom-man threw a hard front kick straight into Bruiser's solar plexus before spinning his rear leg around like a dragon whipping its tail, his heel connecting with Bruiser's temple. The big man fell onto his side. Whether he was out or not, it was difficult to tell in the flickering of the flame. Axiom-man came down with an axe kick on Bruiser's face just in case just as Lady Fire stumbled toward him out of the flame.

Her wings were gone. Smoke curled from her damaged suit. It seemed she was protected overall from burns but that didn't mean she was protected from anything else.

"He . . . killed you," she said.

He walked up to her, put a gentle finger under her chin to raise it up so he could look her in the eye, then said, "No," and struck her as hard as he could between the eyes.

She dropped.

Bruiser was still on the ground.

The fire closed in around them as it ate up more grass.

He could leave them here to burn and the world would be better off for it. Axiom-man turned from them and headed toward the edge of the fire ring. It was fairly thick but perhaps if he ran quick enough through it, he could avoid any major burns.

About to dart into the flames, he stopped. Leaving them would remove them as a hindrance from his fight against Redsaw once Redsaw finally surfaced again. Redsaw was the bigger fight and the most important one. These two, it seemed, were mere lackeys, nothing more. But they would be faithful if Redsaw showed and the fight began anew.

The fire closed in. Axiom-man growled. "Fine," and began pulling out foot after foot of line from his belt.

He'd tie it to them and drag them through. Maybe the burns while doing so would be enough to keep them down, and, as much as he hated the thought, it had to be entertained. If he *shifted* to use his ultra strength, it might draw Redsaw prematurely and his own kindness could be his demise. The strength would make hauling them out easier. Without it . . . they could indeed die.

There was nothing to put out the fire. Soon, if he didn't move, he'd be burned alive.

So would they.

He'd have to *shift*—quick—then *shift* back.

He couldn't be responsible for any more deaths.

Even theirs.

Chapter Twenty-four

The entirety of Owen Tower shook with the latest crash of thunder sounding out of the Doorway of Darkness above. Night Fowler was able to maintain her balance but Gunn stumbled to the side and fell against the wall.

"It's gettin' crazy up there," he said.

"Which is why once you're out, I'm going back up," she said.

"What? You're crazy. And who are you anyway?"

"Just a fowler in the night."

"What's a fowler?"

Idiot.

When they reached floor six Night Fowler's heart sank. The stairs from there downward had collapsed inward and sat in a ruined heap of concrete and steel. Small and minor breaks in the debris were of no help. Neither one of them could tunnel through the openings nor would that be a wise move anyway if the makeshift structure further gave way. Both would be pancakes within a second.

The door to floor six was bent outward inside a buckled doorframe. There was a small gap along the side, just enough for fingers. Gunn stuck his chubby digits in and began to pull.

The door didn't budge.

"Too much pressure on it," she said.

He stopped, gave her a stern eye, and said, "Don't talk to me." He went back to work tugging on the door then, after one hard pull that left his face shining in sweat, the thing budged. He adjusted his stance, found more leverage, and yanked again. The door screeched and opened about a foot.

She didn't say anything and instead moved past him, gave him a slight shove so she'd have some room, then squeezed between the opening. She readied herself, identified the door's center of mass, then launched a hard push kick against the area, slamming the heel of her boot into it. The door moved a couple inches. She kicked it again and again, sending it forward bit by bit until there was enough room for Gunn to get through and onto the floor proper.

"Thanks," he said as he walked past.

Don't mention it.

———

Axiom-man had briefly *shifted* and brought his powers to the fore to get Battle Bruiser and Lady Fire out of the flame. The two were unconscious, injured, and he even went so far as delivering another blow while they were under to keep them that way.

A violent crack of red light burst overhead amidst the red-and-black-clouded sky. Axiom-man looked up to see Redsaw exiting the sky above without the use of a Doorway. How or why he had been able to do that, Axiom-man didn't know nor did he expect himself to. That red-and-black mosaic of a world was Redsaw's domain and who knew what power he was able to exercise within it to enter or exit the realm.

Axiom-man estimated Redsaw was coming in hot at about four hundred kilometers an hour, way too fast to be countered and . . . something must have happened during his absence to make Redsaw so powerful. It seemed the man was already more than when he first fought him atop

Owen Tower and now, perhaps from being inside the Doorway, that power had been amplified to an excessive degree.

He couldn't take Redsaw plowing into him nor was he fast enough to move out of the way at the right moment. At least, not without his abilities. It must have been his briefly turning them on that signaled Redsaw here.

Exhaustion ran through Axiom-man's body. Powered down, it seemed every inch of his flesh was recovering from all that had occurred right before now and the deep thickness of the urge to sleep hung over his eyes and in his head.

Only one way to eliminate it.

Axiom-man *shifted* and powered up. A surge of renewed vigor pumped through his veins. He fired up the power in his eyes. A tidal wave of blue energy tore the air, right at Redsaw. Red fiery blasts of power streamed from Redsaw's fists, clashing with the blue energy and sending a blast of purple light high into the air.

Axiom-man focused and put everything he had behind his eyebeams, shooting out surge after surge of violent energy. From a distance, he sensed Redsaw's resistance through his effort so poured on even more.

Redsaw streaked over the ground, nice and low, the clashing of their blasts chewing up the rocky and muddy ground in an ongoing explosion of rocks and debris the closer he drew near. Redsaw's screams of fury echoed somewhere behind the blast.

Axiom-man shifted the focus to his aura, his black and gray suit covered in a blue sheen of light. A ball of purple energy surged toward him, its enormous size enough to completely engulf him. He dove to the left to miss the impact. Redsaw clipped him on the shoulder as he blasted past, forcing Axiom-man into a spiral in the air.

He kicked on his flight the second he fell from the apex of the strike, threw out both fists before him, and headed as fast as he could muster toward Redsaw in an effort to nail him from behind.

A wall of red energy headed toward him. Redsaw must have turned around.

Axiom-man thought it through: Redsaw's arms would be outstretched, body horizontal, head full of rage and determination.

He took his flight to the limit, pushing over two hundred kliks an hour. Just as he braced for the impact of Redsaw's raw power, he slipped slightly to the side, grabbing Redsaw's wrist as he flew past, locked in his grip, and spun the man around to face the other direction in a violent pull. The second Redsaw was forced to turn, Axiom-man drew in the black-clad wrist in his hand while simultaneously delivering a direct and hard straight punch to Redsaw's nose. His knuckles stung on impact, but it seemed his aura was enough to prevent broken fingers.

Redsaw's head snapped back, the daze from the unexpected blow evident in his eyes. Axiom-man hoped the impact was enough to jar the neck but he couldn't be sure. Two firm hands grabbed his shoulders. Axiom-man tucked his knees up so they stopped Redsaw from pulling him in whatever direction was the goal. Instead, Axiom-man dug his thumbs into the radial nerve on each of Redsaw's forearms, pressed hard, and threw him back and over himself, sending them skidding across the ground. Axiom-man spun in the air and headed straight toward him. Before Redsaw could get up, he received a boot to the face and a fast elbow to the side of the head.

He dropped.

And lay there.

Axiom-man stood over him.

Valerie. He tried to push the thought of her out of his head, tried to remain completely focused on the fight, but with Redsaw down, his headspace began to drift. This man killed Valerie.

Valerie!

Everything shifted before Axiom-man's vision and no longer did he stand over his enemy but instead found himself on one knee beside him, both hands gripped around Redsaw's neck, his thumbs poised to push the larynx straight in for a break that would puncture the esophagus.

Just. One. Violent. Push.

His wrists began to heat up and it was only the increasing heat that pulled him out of the moment. Redsaw squeezed his wrists, the pressure reaching his bones. It wouldn't take much for Redsaw to snap his wrists if he allowed the man to keep his hands there.

But it had to end now.

Had to.

No matter how.

No matter why.

No matter what.

He wanted to call out to Aiyesha and ask what to do, what choice to make, but he knew this time, this moment, was his decision.

Axiom-man wished time would slow, wished there was more time to think it through—but not now. And, most likely, not ever again.

He let blue energy fill and crackle in his eyes, letting it build and build until the power was so great it canceled out his vision. So as not to miss the chance or let Redsaw somehow evade him, Axiom-man closed his mind off to the rest of the world. His heart sank into his stomach, his wrists burning, the pain somehow slowly subsiding as he focused on what he had to do.

He shot out his eyebeams with everything he had, blasting where Redsaw's head had to be, envisioning the man's face burst into oblivion as he finally put an end to the monster's reign of terror and death.

A sudden flash of purple burst before his eyes, sending fiery pain into his eyeballs and eye sockets, seeming to stream straight through and cut into his brain.

What was Redsaw—

Screaming, unable to think, not knowing which way was up or down, Axiom-man fell to the side.

All went dark, then . . .

Awake . . . but nothing but jet black for sight.

The heat returned to his wrists. He could picture his hands melting in his mind's eye.

A rush of speeding air engulfed his body. He threw on his flight to slow the ride but crashed into a pile of rocks anyway.

Ears ringing, head lost to the ruins of impact, sight completely gone, Axiom-man shuddered when, somewhere beyond the auditory ringing, there were footfalls.

All he could do was focus on his aura.

It was his only protection.

The footfalls drew near.

CHAPTER TWENTY-FIVE

THE STORM ABOVE seemed to be getting worse so far as Axiom-man could tell. Booms of raw-powered thunder and the crackling of lightning sounded overhead in a seeming increase of cacophony and chaos.

He just wished he could see it to verify what was going on and adjust his game plan if needed.

A boot knocked him under the chin and sent him backward. He did a break-fall to lessen the impact then put his hands in front of him in a guard for any further incoming.

And it came from the back. Firm fingers gripped him by the back of his neck and lifted him off the ground. He threw a back kick into Redsaw's middle. The man wavered under the impact but his hold didn't relent. Axiom-man threw back two more; the hold released amidst a series of grunts. He spun on his heels, fighting blind, and did a reverse crescent kick to hopefully tag Redsaw across the head. Instead of impact, his leg traveled through the air so he made sure to pull it back in and firmly plant his foot back down.

"Speak," he found himself saying. Speech would give him an idea as to where Redsaw was.

"You're not worth speaking to," Redsaw said. "Never was. Not after all this time. You do not negotiate and neither do I therefore we're at an impasse. We've always been at an impasse."

"And we always will be."

Something came in quick but Axiom-man didn't know what so he asserted his guard and blocked what felt like an incoming fist. He lashed back out at the dark, forgetting to take his time. Redsaw popped him in the mouth then grabbed his arm and hurled him hard through the air, sending him crashing into what felt like a tree but much harder.

Metal.

The humming and slight vibration of the thing sent heat and waves of nausea through him, as if whatever he was against was a conduit it to . . . . He knew exactly where he was.

Bolts of lightning slammed into his aura, each rip into him forcing him to collapse inward and sink down, making himself small. He knew Redsaw was watching, but how long until the man acted, he didn't know.

Axiom-man tried to move—to get out of the fray—but the lightning held him there as if each bolt was a tether to the silver pillars. He knew the layout. He'd seen it before. The pillars interconnected, feeding off each other, exchanging power and also giving power to itself, the almighty Doorway of Darkness above their apex.

A bolt sent him face first into the rock. He heard a tooth crack. Maybe two.

Valerie had been here, in a way, helpless beneath the pillars of darkness and evil whose only function was to serve their creator and open a portal to another dimension.

He saw her, as clear as a picture, bolts of red and impossible heat cooking her, setting her insides aflame and destroying what was left of her beautiful person, her beautiful life.

Inside his heart, the mask fell, and there was only Gabriel, alone, dying, about to be destroyed by the very thing he had fought against his entire time in the cape. The very person he trained to overcome. The very person who threatened the entire world.

The thickness of the illness Redsaw's power produced made Axiom-man no more than a helpless boy drowning in a lake in the middle of the night with no one around to pull him out.

It was like being in that coffin again but this time, much worse.

————

Before . . . at the Central, early on, the wooden board. Straight punch. Knuckles to rope. Over and over.

Aiyesha spoke from behind. "Your form has improved but your inner form has not."

Gabriel kept punching. "Inner form?"

"You are viewing your strikes as a task, an item to be done. This is why you are beginning to get bored despite what we're doing."

She had him there. One could only punch an object over and over for so long until boredom began to set in.

"And you're trying to prove a point," she said, "which is then missing the point of what we are doing here today."

He punched once more then lowered his hand. "Then what am I missing?"

"I didn't say you could stop." Her voice was firm.

"I'm sorry, Mistress." He resumed striking, blood beginning to trickle down his knuckles.

"When you strike, it is more than just an action. It is an intent, an expression of yourself. That which is within will manifest through your movement and will inform your technique, precision, and power. Until you align yourself and draw from deep within yourself with intent, you will never break that board."

He hit it harder. The board took it just fine.

"Stop and turn around," she said.

He did.

"Look into my eyes."

He did.

She held his gaze, her face stoic, her body calm and unreadable.

The two remained that way for a few minutes before Gabriel's gaze began to drift to the right.

"What are you looking at?" she said. "I'm over here."

"Sorry, Mistress."

"Focus. Look at my eyes. Concentrate . . . and let go."

He held her green eyes in sight of his own. There was a hardness in those eyes yet a sense of care.

He tensed, waiting for her to make a move on him.

Her eyes didn't waiver. "Breathe."

He obeyed. He always obeyed. Each slow breath brought him closer and closer to center.

He lost track of time as the two remained looking into each other's eyes.

Green, like bright emeralds, cosmic stars amidst a calm face and jet black hair and a completely relaxed body.

Green.

Easy to get lost in.

So lost . . . so . . .

"Gabriel," she said.

"Yes, Mistress."

"Look."

He furrowed his brow . . . then saw it. His left forearm was up, her wrist crossing with it, her fist just past that.

He didn't recall her striking.

He didn't recall blocking.

She eyed where their limbs met and didn't withdraw.

"How . . . ?" he started but didn't really know what he was trying to ask.

"Intent," she said. "Intent."

––––––––––

I could go in and ensure he doesn't survive, Redsaw thought. Except . . . watching Axiom-man being pummelled by shocks of violent red energy was very satisfying. Yet, if he let the red power do its work, by proxy it would be his master who put an end to him, not himself. And, after all this time, after all this struggle, after defeating that "Axiom" man then having him return, for someone else to see to it this man was no longer a problem was unacceptable.

He wanted to bring Axiom-man's head to his master and finally get what was his.

Redsaw drew close.

––––––––––

Axiom-man, beaten to the point where all he could do was rest on his forearms and knees, each slam of red power sending a shockwave of pain through his body and twisting his insides into a taut spiraled rope that wouldn't relent, was lost in the heavy black of its chaos.

Darkness all around.

The coffin.

So hopeless and futile yet . . . he had got out. But here, this wasn't some wooden box. This was jail. Permanent jail. And this time . . . this time he might actually die.

Axiom-man slowed his breath, picked a spot in the pitch black before his vision and focused on that piece of darkness alone. Slowly, and oh so carefully, he pushed himself to cross the line of defense and resistance to acceptance.

Let it beat down. Let it come.

Let go.

"Just . . . let . . . go," he whispered. *Valerie. Mom. My family. Oh no . . .*

Slow. Breathe. Ignore the heat and the sharp stench of fiery metal. Focus on the dark.

The black.

The nothing.

Let go.

. . .

. . .

. . .

A glimmer of bright blue flickered against the black backdrop of his vision. It flashed as if a wisp of vapor drifting apart. Another flash, more blue, the vapor.

The loose outline of a face.

The face that had no name.

The face that . . . had *his* name: Axiom-man.

He saw himself in the dark, looking back at him, eyes of blue energy gazing at him and never breaking hold.

Axiom-man wasn't sure, but he might have been forced to *shift* down. He didn't know. And he was just Gabriel in a costume.

Gabriel held Axiom-man's gaze, his eyes never wavering from that strange light blue silhouette amidst the dark. That face. That mask. Those powers.

The vast void of darkness between him and what he had become when the messenger first visited him all that time ago.

He could let it all go here. Let Axiom-man go.

Let everything go.

There was nothing outside this place of darkness and blue light. He knew there was something . . . but it felt like nothing. Another world, maybe? A person? He couldn't be sure.

The pain from the energy blasts had ceased and he had lost track as to when.

If this was death, then he would let it come.

He held Axiom-man's gaze.

And let go.

———

A violent flash of bright blue light and power sent Redsaw flying back from the glowing red pillars and cast him tumbling along the rocky ground. When he glanced up, he was at least a hundred feet away and no matter which way he tried, he couldn't get his feet under him.

"What the—"

He looked to the Doorway . . . and his eyes widened when he saw a man in blue light floating between the pillars.

———

The hard surface of silver met Axiom-man's palms on either side of him. Blue light and cracks of light blue lightning snapped and sped all around him in a ripping tornado of raw energy.

Through the light, just barely, he caught sight of his hands against the metal . . . and the black and gray of his suit gone.

In his peripheral, he noticed a long light blue cape draped over his shoulders. He gazed downward and saw his standard uniform but this time coated in a flurry of sparkling blue energy, the ground far beneath his feet.

Inside, a surge of ferocious energy burst through him and all he could do was throw his head to the sky and with a scream that echoed across the area, let loose a massive blast of crystal blue energy straight into where the pillars met. Pressing outward against them as hard as he could, he pushed against the pillars, his eyebeams destroying their connection at the top.

Somewhere far away: "No. Stop!"

With a ferocious growl, Axiom-man pressed all the way outward while surge after surge of blue energy spilled from his eyes and pierced the beams and Doorway above.

With a gust of effort, he shoved the pillars away from each other. They hurtled through the air, the entire structure dispersed.

Above, the raucous bang of thunder after thunder yelled across the land.

Axiom-man rose up and blasted straight through the Doorway's opening. Ascending from bottom to top, his body ripped through the frame. Explosions of red energy tore across the land, his blue power utterly decimating the open door. Now, high in the sky, his vision began to clear as the massive Doorway that covered all began to recede south at breakneck speed.

Axiom-man streaked after it.

CHAPTER TWENTY-SIX

THE ENTIRE SILVER structure was in a heap upon the rocks, the beams still glowing red with heat but not nearly enough to awaken the Doorway of Darkness.

Redsaw glanced up and watched as if through foggy eyes as the giant door over the land raced south across the sky, closing, a fine beam of bright blue light trailing after it.

It was *him,* he thought. "It was him." He looked to the hill, to the sky, to the ground. "It. Was. Him!"

With a ferocious growl, Redsaw tore off into the sky after Axiom-man. He had always been faster so he'd catch up eventually, and when he did, he would kill him and would steal every shred of the man's power. He would end this stupid dance they've been conducting for so long. He would end that rotten do-gooder always screwing up his plans.

There would be blood.

Lots of blood.

———

Axiom-man sped through the air like a spear going hard after its target. The thunderous Doorway above receded like a scroll, each pull revealing more and more of the evening sky. But it was fast. Man, was it fast.

Axiom-man kicked on the speed as much as he could, noticing he flew faster than usual. Not insanely faster but at least a hundred or a hundred and fifty kliks an hour more.

But the Doorway was faster, and he could only assume the peal-back above was heading back to the Doorway atop Owen Tower. Once it arrived and what it might do, he didn't know. All that was important was to try to stop it. He could only imagine if the storm above crashed back into the Doorway, the effect of the impact could be enough to shake every building downtown to the ground. Not that many were left standing as it was.

Pushing himself, he managed to go a little faster. But only a little. Inside, he sensed something not adding up. He couldn't quite place it but something wasn't right inside. An injury? No. He'd feel the pain or the discomfort. He was hurt, sure, but not in the way he sought. Everything just felt *off* and out of alignment. This moment, this care, this effort—all of it didn't seem to be operating the way it should be. The problem was, he didn't know what this *should be* should be.

A swell of anger bubbled up within along with a surge of frustration. This was new. He knew the difference between something not going his way or getting out of control—lots of experience with that—but this sensation of things not locking in made him yell against the sky as he flew.

He kept his flight line straight but closed his eyes a moment, tried to quiet his mind. Tried to even ignore the claps of thunder off in the distance from the receding Doorway.

He thought back to the surge of power that filled him when he transformed. Thought back to separating the pillars and breaking their feed into the main Doorway.

That moment. That was the moment, he thought. *Aiyesha. Her lesson. Her reason. Her* intent.

"Let go," he said quietly. *Let go.*

He opened his eyes, narrowed them, and fixed them on the receding Doorway. Below, prairie fields raced in a blur as he flew over them, but it wasn't fast enough.

Let go.

What felt like a violent ongoing push from behind sent him streaking through the air, his speed increasing by leaps and bounds. He couldn't put a label on the actual speed but this was at least double. Maybe triple. But oh so very quickly he was almost beneath the Doorway.

He relaxed even more. Let go even further . . . and flew faster.

————

Redsaw suddenly stopped and hovered midair when the spark of blue light in the distance flashed out of existence. Did the Doorway somehow take Axiom-man out? Swallowed him whole?

He adjusted himself, arms outstretched, and moved as quickly as he could through the air.

He had to know if Axiom-man was alive. He had to know if the Doorway of Darkness on top of his building was okay.

Had to know he still had the opportunity to kill.

————

Axiom-man's aura pulsed around him as he sped through the air. No longer was it a fine sheen of light over his entire body but a powerful glow of bright blue power, a shield against anything sent his way, including the immense rush of wind plowing into him as he rocketed through the air. Before, at the beginning when he first got his powers, he had to fly keeping his mouth pointed downward so he wouldn't choke on the speeding air entering his lungs. Now, he breathed just fine and smiled beneath his mask at the revelation. He reached up to the top if his head and felt the fabric from what was once his dark suit covering his head in full. He grabbed hold of the material and tore it, leaving a hole for his bright blue hair to flow out.

He focused on the speed, on the retreating massive Doorway, and headed right for the city where the Doorway spiraled atop the pyramid structure of silver pillars, forcing a storm to form above it.

He would not let the Doorway of Darkness poison the world again. Not after today. He already experienced the immense damage the original opening years back caused, the lingering black clouds' ability to transport himself and others to different worlds, random traps set throughout the city and beyond for any poor soul who might stumble across one and fall victim to its pull.

Axiom-man brought his fists together as the top of Owen Tower neared along with the pillars that joined at their peak. Eyes fixed, will strong, Axiom-man aimed directly for them. They'd be destroyed and hopefully this Doorway of Darkness would close.

Fifty feet.

Ten.

Five.

Impact in . . . . A violent red lightning bolt shot out of the Doorway and crashed into him, sending a shockwave through his body from the impact. The aura absorbed a good portion of the blow but it was still enough to throw him off course and tumbling backward through the air.

No matter.

He righted himself and cranked on the speed again, determined to smash through the pillars and put an end to the madness once and for all.

The second he was about to make contact, a double streak of lightning surged from the Doorway and plowed into him again.

This time, a wave of dizziness filled his head from the impact and a dull ache spread over his body.

"Point taken," he said, "but not valid." Filling his eyes with as much power as he could muster, he pointed himself like an arrow in the air and flew full force toward the pillars some half a kilometer away. Giving it all he had, he took his speed to a full out air sprint and shot his energy beams directly at the top of the pillars to weaken them.

Violent bursts of purple light where blue and red met shot in all directions as his power clashed with the Doorway's.

With a screaming shout, Axiom-man drew his hands together and plowed into the beams, breaking through them and sending shards of silver in a dance of debris into the air.

A horrendously loud boom of thunder erupted from the Doorway. On the streets below, echo after echo of bursting glass tore from the remainder of the surrounding buildings. A body-shaking rumble of an earthquake roared through the city streets, upending the concrete and creating a spider web of large, deep cracks in the ground.

Axiom-man turned in the air and headed back to Owen Tower. Once the remains of the pillars came into view, he noticed they were still feeding the Doorway but not nearly as efficiently as before. The Doorway above bent and twisted and groaned as it fought to remain open.

"I have to take the whole place down," he said as got ready to do just that.

Wait. To the side.

Axiom-man pivoted in the air and caught Redsaw over the arms as his enemy slammed into him and wrapped his arms around Axiom-man's middle.

Before Axiom-man could dig in, jerk his hands up, and snap some of Redsaw's ribs, the two plowed into an adjacent building, crashing through the wall, speeding across a blur of messy office space before smashing through the wall on the opposite side.

Axiom-man took hold, jerked their bodies backward, and hurled Redsaw up and over himself and into a support pillar of a parkade beyond.

Without missing a beat, Axiom-man headed straight toward him. He could have gone after the Doorway first but Redsaw would no doubt interfere. Efficiency.

Redsaw recovered and darted at him, a streak of red through the air.

The two collided.

CHAPTER TWENTY-SEVEN

SLAMMING INTO AXIOM-MAN was like crashing into a tank. This wasn't right. This wasn't how it was supposed to go. Axiom-man had always been the lesser and now . . . now it seemed that despite Redsaw's own upgrades, whatever was powering Axiom-man exceeded it.

Doesn't matter, Redsaw thought, but deep down he knew that, right now, it *did* matter.

Bring him here, his master said within.

Redsaw nodded to himself then tore after Axiom-man, entangling their arms so he could drag the man in blue to the contorting Doorway above the tower. Axiom-man removed control from the hold and inflicted his own. Redsaw's face lit up in fresh pain as a cheekbone broke from what felt like a series of at least five blows done in quick succession.

He swung out and his fist whipped through nothing but air.

A strike caught him at the base of his skull and his world momentarily flashed dark before blurring then clearing again.

Axiom-man had let go of his arm.

Redsaw faced the Doorway and blue light burst near it. He flew toward it only to see it was just a blast that forced purple light along one of the Doorway's sides.

"Bastard," he muttered. He turned around, expecting a surprise attack from behind but instead saw nothing but the smoky and dusty air that hovered over the city.

His bottom teeth slammed into his upper teeth. The clashing teeth created a series of cracking sounds as his jaw shattered. Something struck the lower half of his face from below. His head snapped back from the impact, throwing his neck out of joint. He tried to right himself and put his hands up with fists alit with red.

Axiom-man was nowhere in sight.

"Come on!" Redsaw shouted into the air. "Coward! Face me!" But the words were feeble. Axiom-man had taken the power in his voice.

A strange low whistle droned on the air, seeming to come from the right but its sound was hard to pinpoint.

Axiom-man came in like a missile and interlocked his arms with Redsaw's shoulders, and try as Redsaw did against this strange blue light surrounding Axiom-man's body, every blow seemed to be a light tap for Axiom-man.

For the first time in years, Redsaw's heart picked up pace.

————

Night Fowler pried open the elevator doors inside Owen Tower. The other stairwell was blocked by heavy debris on the other side of the door. Once the elevator door was open, she shone a flashlight up and down the shaft to get an idea as to where the elevator was. She caught sight of what she figured was its underside some twelve or fifteen floors above.

Gunn came beside her. "What're you doing?"

"Working." She clamped a small, black rectangular box with rollers on the main pulley inside the elevator. She then grabbed Gunn by the arm and pulled him to the elevator door's edge.

"Hey, watch it!" he said.

Shut up. She grabbed his suspenders from the front, drawing the bands together, then pulled them tight and close a few inches above his belt. She clasped the device to his suspenders with him holding arms out to the side and looking down, seemingly allowing her to do her work.

"I don't like this," he said.

"You don't have to. Get to the bottom, get out, make sure the surrounding area is clear of all civilians."

"And who made you captain?"

She didn't answer and instead shoved him into the elevator shaft. Gunn let out a yelp as he dangled there midair, attached to the center pulley.

As Night Fowler turned away from the opening, she reveled in the fading scream as Gunn descended quickly to the ground floor.

She forgot to show him how to undo the device. Not a problem. Pretty sure Gunn was smart enough to take his suspenders off.

Hopefully.

Axiom-man twisted Redsaw's body around and positioned them both in the air, his sights set to about three quarters up Owen Tower.

Redsaw's fists alit with red energy. Wasting no time, Axiom-man blocked the attempted blow to his face and redirected Redsaw's fists toward the building the moment energy poured out. Cranking on his flight full speed, Axiom-man shot energy beams from his eyes, directing both his and Redsaw's power toward his target.

The second the beams made impact, the side of Owen Tower exploded in a spray of brick and steel and glass.

Dragging Redsaw along with as much force as he could, Axiom-man sent them both through the building, deliberately crashing into the structural support beams.

They were already out the other side of the building. The whole structure began to waver and the Doorway of Darkness above groaned as if it felt the impact too.

"What are you doing!" Redsaw mumbled.

Patience gone, Axiom-man punched his nose and steered them both back into the building, taking out another support pillar.

Redsaw heated up his hands and tried to burn Axiom-man anywhere and everywhere he might find a spot, but the blue aura fought against the red power in those hands, rendering the effort useless. Axiom-man pulled him down through another floor of the building. As they broke through on the other side, Axiom-man kept Aiyesha's advice about maintaining momentum at the fore of his mind. He turned them both around again and hurled their bodies back through the building.

Adjusting his hold and now taking Redsaw by the cape, he yanked upward on the material, hoping the cowl and cape combination would create a noose around Redsaw's neck.

Axiom-man wrapped his hands within the fabric of the black cape so all was good and solid then spun in the air as fast as he could, building up speed and momentum. He threw Redsaw across the top of Owen Tower into the remains of the silver pillars, destroying them further. The Doorway above flickered.

Redsaw's body fell onto his throne and the man lay there in a heap.

Axiom-man had to confirm the kill but before he could get close, the entire building buckled and groaned.

———

Gunn had taken a pocket knife to his suspenders to get the contraption that made him piss his pants on the way down off his body. Pants now wet and cold, he hated every scrambling step to get out of the building, and he swore if he ever came across that coo-coo person in dark gray again, he'd figure out a way to make them pee their own pants.

Echoing in low hums and booms from somewhere on the floors above, Gunn knew the sound meant nothing good was about to happen.

He saw the front entrance and the rubble on the other side. But he spied an opening. Top right corner. An area of glass unimpeded by the stacked debris beyond. He drew his weapon and fired at it; the glass shattered and rained to the ground, giving access to the mountain of wreckage beyond.

Gunn scrambled to the foot of the pile and drew a deep breath. *Climb, get out, run.* Basic plan.

Gunn took hold of what appeared to be the best choice of concrete debris to hold his weight and started to climb.

———

Night Fowler took a hard look up the elevator shaft to see if there was an opening somewhere high up that might lead to the roof. But it was too dark and the beam of her flashlight didn't reach high enough to suggest any possibilities. With a grunt, she headed to the window and noticed the vast expanse of a red and black sky no longer reigned over the land.

Axiom-man? she thought. Had he done it? Was it over? How could she miss—

The building swayed and thunderous bangs sounded on distant floors above. She placed a gloved palm to the wall.

It vibrated.

"Oh crap," she said.

———

The entirety of Owen Tower began to sway and then, for a moment, was utterly still.

"Oh man," Axiom-man breathed.

In an instant, one floor gave out and the entire top third of the building dropped straight down on itself, sending out a spray of dust and brick.

He eyed Redsaw, who was straightening himself on his throne.

Axiom-man sped in and slammed him against the chair, decked him in the mouth, then nailed him deliberately just above the chin to trigger a cluster of nerves.

Redsaw slumped. Above, the Doorway twisted in the air, its frame sending out bolts of red lightning and oozing gusts of black clouds.

Axiom-man hoisted Redsaw off his throne and took him straight up toward the Doorway. He held Redsaw in front of it.

"Here, this is yours!" he said and hurled Redsaw through the air and into the Doorway.

Axiom-man turned to fly away and two long electric strings of red power wrapped around his body, pulling him toward the Doorway. He glanced over his shoulder.

Redsaw was conscious. Maybe throwing him in there hadn't been a wise idea.

Redsaw pulled him in as if fighting to reel in a catch. Axiom-man pulled against the restraints, dragging himself forward through the air, attempting to break free.

A powerful tug surprised him and jerked him back.

He fought against his bonds, desperately trying to not get drawn into that place of darkness. He didn't know the extent of his new power and how it would hold up within that realm.

But he knew something now and recognized it was something he had to figure out for himself all this time. Aiyesha was just a prompter. *Intent.* The source of one's will. The heart of one's motive. The purpose for doing anything.

And the way to make his powers work together instead of separately. If he could now fly at at least four hundred kilometers an hour, that suggested he could move at that rate too. What did it matter if he used the speed for flight or for something else?

In case he was wrong, he cautiously focused and put on the flight, this time spinning his body as he did so, coiling and tightening the red energy beams around him. He spun in place, faster and faster.

The red strands of power crackled and sparked. He blasted energy from his eyes, spinning and spinning and cutting into his bonds. The tension pulling against him released and a bright burst of purple splashed outward in majestic rays of energy.

With all he had, he headed straight for Redsaw, who was coming out of the Doorway. Axiom-man crossed his arms in front of his face as Redsaw hurled bolt after bolt at him. His aura absorbed the blows . . . but it still stung his arms. The second Redsaw reached the edge of the

Doorway, Axiom-man flew in hard with a deadly straight punch and slammed Redsaw in the heart. The man in red and black hurtled backward far into the Doorway's realm.

Axiom-man dove straight down onto the teetering building, smashing through Redsaw's throne and plowing through floor after floor to take the place out.

———

Night Fowler clung to the side of the building, her line anchored a few floors above. Walls blew out beside her and below her.

Her line went slack.

She fell.

———

Gunn had rolled down the hill of debris just outside the building entrance and lay face first on the pavement.

"Get up, you fat bastard. Move!" he told himself.

He pushed himself onto cut-up palms and sore feet, centered his head, then stood.

A violent crash above; he looked up.

The entire building collapsed downward.

It was too late.

Just as the third floor busted outward, a streak of blue light sped out of the building and grabbed him under the arms. He shrieked as his feet suddenly left the pavement.

The ground buckled and shook as Owen Tower fell behind them, an enormous dust cloud firing out in all directions, bathing everything in his sight in a hurricane of brown and gray dust. He snapped his mouth shut when his tongue went dry from the dust and pinched his nose.

The only problem was, he forgot to take a breath before he did so. The pressure in his lungs quickly built, and he wanted to gasp for air but forced himself to keep his mouth clamped shut.

Eyes closed, sharp flying debris poked at his face like needles. He'd be surprised if he still had a face after this.

It hurt. His chest. He had to breathe. Air. Now!

He coughed and gagged but the air was relatively clean. The ground came up to meet him fast.

Set on his feet, he squinted through blurry vision to see a familiar blue figure race away from him back into the fray.

"Well, I'll be" —he coughed up a wad of dust— "well, I'll be damned." *You're back.*

―――――

Axiom-man used his energy beams to help him navigate the darkness of the dust cloud. He couldn't see Redsaw anywhere. He looked for the Doorway and couldn't see that either. And he couldn't wait for the dust to settle before confirming the threat was over.

Might as well do it again, he thought. Quickly, he began to spin, ripping himself around at top speed as he ascended higher and higher, creating a kind of wind funnel for the dust to follow. He didn't know how well he was doing but he had to try. He gave it all he had. He spun and spun and flew and flew, drawing the chaos into the sky.

When he stopped, he had to be at least fifteen or twenty thousand feet up. A huge spiral of dust followed him. He dove back down, following the funnel and landed on a foggy street.

"Now we know for next time," he told himself. *Better not be a next time.*

At ground level, Owen Tower sat in a heap of ruin, the mound of broken building and debris several storeys high.

The Doorway of Darkness was not above it.

Nor was Redsaw.

Nor was anything but dusty sky filled with plumes of dirt and smoke.

He committed to staying there for as long as necessary until he was sure Redsaw was indeed gone.

Epilogue

GABRIEL COULDN'T BRING himself to visit Valerie's grave. Oh, he wanted to. Wanted to stand there and cry, collapse and pour his heart out, kiss the ground and, if it weren't so extreme, claw his way through the earth just to be with her. But that life was gone. He had tried to so hard to get her attention back at Dolla-card. Tried too hard to be a good friend while still being Axiom-man.

She had found out about him before he told her. And now . . . that secret was with her in this grave, gone forever from the world.

He had let her down. Not just with her death but with focusing so hard on ending Redsaw's presence on this earth that he didn't properly mourn her. Properly grieve.

Maybe that's what this was about now, the not visiting. Maybe he just needed some time, and then, one day, he would go and tell her whatever needed to be said. He just hoped that when she passed, she didn't think he had failed her. Valerie understood the mission despite its cost. That's why she supported him when everything went downhill and he had no place to go and nothing to offer anyone other than being Axiom-man.

She died a hero.

Night Fowler was missing. Gabriel had followed the news as the City crews worked night and day to clear away the remains of Owen Tower. Part of the cleanup involved finding casualties in the rubble and no bodies were found.

None.

Though a relief, Gabriel had seen Katie pull this trick before. She'd turn up. One day.

The media kept playing clips on the search for Oscar Owen. The man would no doubt have come out of hiding to comment on the destruction of his empire. According to reports, no one answered his phone and a search of his mansion revealed he wasn't there either. The media figured he might be abroad on business and hadn't yet learned what happened. Unlikely, but possible.

But Gabriel knew. It was the only thing that made sense. He remembered pealing back Redsaw's mask to a beaten-up face beneath. It could have been him. The hair matched. The skin color that wasn't bruised and bloody matched as well.

Gabriel would keep an eye and ear out just in case, but he was pretty sure this world had seen the last of Redsaw and the man beneath the cowl.

But Winnipeg would never be the same. Half the city was destroyed. Crime was rampant. Chaos ruled the streets because most of the city was a wasteland.

Battle Bruiser and Lady Fire were on the lam. They'd turn up too and Gabriel would put them away. As for Bleaken—the fight with Redsaw left so much unattended. He couldn't be everywhere at once nor do it all at once. He did what needed doing and that was eliminate the most dangerous threat.

Gabriel looked out the glassless window of Valerie's apartment. Her suite had survived but the building was deemed unstable and tenants were asked to make alternate arrangements. Where everyone would go was anyone's guess.

There was no word from Aiyesha or the messenger. It was almost as if what he accomplished wasn't worthy of notice from them. But that was also them and who they were.

Things would straighten out. Eventually. Just not today.

When a siren rose in the distance, Gabriel smirked and unbuttoned his shirt, revealing his Axiom-man uniform beneath.

At least one side of him had a job. He let the clothes fall to a heap on the floor and *shifted* as he pulled his mask on.

Things seemed somehow complete despite work still needing to be done and, for now, he was more than willing to pitch in.

Axiom-man stepped up onto the railing of Valerie's balcony, put his arms out beside him and tipped forward, falling before kicking on the flight before impact and swooping up to meet the sky.

That fall, that swoop.

He loved that part.

About the Author

A.P. Fuchs is the author of many novels and short stories. His most recent books are *Axiom-man/Crimson Cloak: Scarlet Synergy*, *Zomtropolis: A Record of Life in a Dead City*, and *Giganti-gator Death Machine: Triple Feature*.

Also a cartoonist, he is known for his superhero series, *The Axiom-man Saga*, both in novel and comic book format. Please visit **www.canisterx.com** for more on this series. For his webcomic, *Fredrikus*, about a down-and-out anthropomorphic dog in a dystopian sci-fi world, please go to **www.fredrikus.com**

As well, be sure to subscribe to A.P. Fuchs's YouTube Channel at **www.youtube.com/@apfuchs** for books, comics, podcasts, stories, and more.